The Cheyenne

The Cheyenne

Gwen Remington

Lucent Books, Inc.
P.O. Box 289011, San Diego, California

Titles in the Indigenous Peoples of North America Series Include:

Library of Congress Cataloging-in-Publication Data

Remington, Gwen, 1956–
    The Cheyenne / by Gwen Remington.
        p. cm. — (Indigenous peoples of North America)
Includes bibliographical references and index.
Summary: Discusses the Cheyenne Native Americans including their
nomadic life, social and religious customs, peace chiefs and war
leaders, wars, early days on the reservation, and current situation.
    ISBN 1-56006-750-0
    1. Cheyenne Indians—Juvenile literature. [1. Cheyenne Indians.
2. Indians of North America—Great Plains.] I. Title. II. Series.
    E99.C53 R44 2001
    978.004'973—dc21

                                                    00-008653

Copyright 2001 by Lucent Books, Inc.
P.O. Box 289011, San Diego, California 92198-9011

Printed in the U.S.A.

Contents

Foreword

North America's native peoples are often relegated to history—viewed primarily as remnants of another era—or cast in the stereotypical images long found in popular entertainment and even literature. Efforts to characterize Native Americans typically result in idealized portrayals of spiritualists communing with nature or bigoted descriptions of savages incapable of living in civilized society. Lost in these unfortunate images is the rich variety of customs, beliefs, and values that comprised—and still comprise—many of North America's native populations.

The *Indigenous Peoples of North America* series strives to present a complex, realistic picture of the many and varied Native American cultures. Each book in the series offers historical perspectives as well as a view of contemporary life of individual tribes and tribes that share a common region. The series examines traditional family life, spirituality, interaction with other native and non-native peoples, warfare, and the ways the environment shaped the lives and cultures of North America's indigenous populations. Each book ends with a discussion of life today for the Native Americans of a given region or tribe.

In any discussion of the Native American experience, there are bound to be sim-

ilarities. All tribes share a past filled with unceasing white expansion and resistance that led to more than four hundred years of conflict. One U.S. administration after another pursued this goal and fought Indians who attempted to defend their homelands and ways of life. Although no war was ever formally declared, the U.S. policy of conquest precluded any chance of white and Native American peoples living together peacefully. Between 1780 and 1890, Americans killed hundreds of thousands of Indians and wiped out whole tribes.

The Indians lost the fight for their land and ways of life, though not for lack of bravery, skill, or a sense of purpose. They simply could not contend with the overwhelming numbers of whites arriving from Europe or the superior weapons they brought with them. Lack of unity also contributed to the defeat of the Native Americans. For most, tribal identity was more important than racial identity. This loyalty left the Indians at a distinct disadvantage. Whites had a strong racial identity and they fought alongside each other even when there was disagreement because they shared a racial destiny.

Although all Native Americans share this tragic history they have many distinct differences. For example, some tribes and individuals sought to cooperate almost immediately with the U.S. government while others steadfastly resisted the white presence. Life before the arrival of white settlers also varied. The nomads of the Plains developed altogether different lifestyles and customs from the fishermen of the Northwest coast.

Contemporary life is no different in this regard. Many Native Americans—forced onto reservations by the American government—struggle with poverty, poor health, and inferior schooling. But others have regained a sense of pride in themselves and their heritage, enabling them to search out new routes to self-sufficiency and prosperity.

The *Indigenous Peoples of North America* series attempts to capture the differences as well as similarities that make up the experiences of North America's native populations—both past and present. Fully documented primary and secondary source quotations enliven the text. Sidebars highlight events, personalities, and traditions. Bibliographies provide readers with ideas for further research. In all, each book in this dynamic series provides students with a wealth of information as well as launching points for further research.

Tsistsista, the People

The ancestors of the Cheyenne called themselves Tsistsista: the People. They were a small tribe—from 1780 to 1930, their population averaged only three thousand. Their territory, however, was vast. The Tsistsista made camp from the frigid Montana plains to the arid Texas Panhandle, from the pine-covered Rocky Mountains to the grass-carpeted Kansas and Nebraska prairies. General Philip Henry Sheridan declared them the most formidable of all the Plains tribes, warning his superiors in the War Department not to underestimate them. He was right to advise caution. During the Indian Wars of the nineteenth century, the Tsistsista did more to thwart the white man's advances than any other single tribe.

The Tsistsista spoke a strange language, a dialect of Algonquian. The Sioux could not understand them when they first met. They called the Tsistsista *Shahiyena*, which means "foreign speakers." By the time the first white fur traders visited the outskirts of the Great Plains, the wide-ranging and fierce Tsistsista had become known to all as the Cheyenne.

From Lake People to Riverine People

Because the Cheyenne lacked a written language, little is known of their early history, and researchers must look to their spoken language for clues about their tribe. John H. Moore, author of *The Cheyenne*, writes, "Evidence indicates that the Cheyennes are among the Algonquian peoples of North America, and that they originated in the subarctic."[1] This assertion places the earliest Cheyenne in Canada. Oral tradition related by nineteenth-century Cheyenne elders maintains that the tribe once dwelt on the shores of a great lake, perhaps Lake Superior. There they lived in bark-covered huts, subsisting on a diet of fish and skunks. They were a poor people then. When by accident they discovered a better life, in present-day Wisconsin, the Cheyenne took the first small step in a long journey west.

It is in Wisconsin that the Cheyenne are first mentioned by early European explorers. Cheyenne historian Donald J. Berthrong explains:

> Cheyennes appear originally in historical records on a map attributed to Joliet and drawn, perhaps, before 1673. The map places the "Chaiena," or Cheyenne, fifth in a list of tribes living above the mouth of the Wisconsin River and north of the Sioux, thus occupying a portion of the Wisconsin bank of the Mississippi River.[2]

By the late seventeenth century, then, the Cheyenne had evolved from lake people to riverine people. They fished, farmed, and hunted. Their bellies were full, and they were kept warm with animal skins. They were content to settle in one place.

They were not yet warriors, though. When the Cree and the Assiniboin received guns in trade from the Europeans, they began to harass the Cheyenne. Armed only with primitive weapons, the Cheyenne headed west again. They built villages on the border of present-day Minnesota and South Dakota. Once again, hostile tribes forced them to leave these villages behind. They moved to eastern North Dakota and settled along the Sheyenne River, where they built a sturdy village. By 1750 the Algonquian Chippewa claim to have destroyed this village, and the Cheyenne moved again, this time to the western Dakotas near the northern Missouri River.

From Riverine People to Great Plains Warriors

Step by step, the Cheyenne moved west. Before them lay the central Great Plains, a country they were destined to rule. They were an intelligent people, able to learn quickly from experience and observation, and as they progressed, they put their native intelligence to good use. They studied the land and observed its inhabitants,

Cheyenne chiefs like Wolf Robe led the tribe across the Great Plains.

learning to survive in each new environment. Along the way, they became acquainted with two animals that forever changed their lives: the horse and the buffalo. The horse empowered them, awakening the warrior within. The buffalo fed them and kept them warm.

The Cheyenne met many tribes along the way. A small band of Sioux accompanied them across Minnesota and North Dakota, intermarrying with the Cheyenne. They met the Suhtai, distant kin whom they absorbed into their ranks. There were the Teton Sioux, at first hostile but later allies. Ultimately, there were the Arapaho, with whom the Cheyenne became inextricably bound. "With the Arapahoes the Cheyennes became close friends at their first meeting," states George Bent, the son of a fur trader and a Cheyenne woman, "and from then until today [early 1900s] the Cheyennes and Arapahoes are always spoken of together."[3]

The Cheyenne resided for a while with the Mandan and Arikara tribes of the northern Missouri River. These riverine tribes had the white man's guns and iron tools, more than they needed. They also had an abundance of produce such as pumpkins and corn. However, as sedentary

The Lisbon, North Dakota, Site

The Cheyenne took a lengthy break in their migration when they settled on the Sheyenne River in eastern North Dakota near the present-day town of Lisbon. An early-twentieth-century excavation of this site revealed a wealth of information about their stay, which probably occurred during the first half of the eighteenth century.

The Lisbon site was a permanent village located at the top of the Sheyenne riverbank. The village was well fortified from hostile intruders. On one side lay the steep bank and the river, on the other, ditches and other man-made barriers. Between these lay the village, a cluster of round earthen lodges ranging in diameter from forty to sixty feet.

Archaeological evidence found at the site gives experts clues about the Cheyenne lifestyle. Excavators found hoes made of buffalo bones, so it can be assumed that the Cheyenne were already hunting buffalo. They also discovered grinding stones to sharpen hoes; pottery indicating a stable, sedentary life; and evidence that corn, squash, and beans were a central staple of the Cheyenne's diet. There were stone-headed weapons, as well, and a notable absence of the white man's guns.

A Cheyenne woman stands near a horse and a rack of drying buffalo meat while her husband poses in front of their tepee. Horses and buffalo played a vital role in Cheyenne society.

tribes, they lacked horses and buffalo meat and hides. The Cheyenne saw an opportunity. They became traders, the middlemen of the Plains. With the guns, tools, and produce of the Mandan and Arikara, the Cheyenne traveled south to trade these goods for horses. Along the way, they hunted buffalo whenever possible, amassing huge quantities of dried buffalo meat and tanned buffalo hides. Driving herds of horses before them, their own mounts laden with meat and hides, they returned to the north.

The final step in the Cheyenne's long journey as a people was a leap between two diverse cultures: settled and nomadic. Earthen lodges were replaced by those made of skin, farming implements by the gun. The Cheyenne became true nomads; travel their way of life. Because of the horse and the buffalo, the Cheyenne were now warriors, masters of their lands, and they remained unyielding before hostile forces. It soon became known that one did not traverse the central Great Plains without first answering to the Cheyenne.

Chapter 1

The Nomadic Life

The Great Plains of North America are an enormous oblong stretch of land sweeping from Alberta, Canada, in the north to Texas in the south. At their eastern edge lie fertile prairies, a land thickly carpeted with tall, native grasses that dip and rise beneath moderate winds. At their western edge the magnificent Rocky Mountain range sketches a jagged horizon. In the center of the Great Plains lies the country known as the central high plains. Elliot West, author of *The Contested Plains: Indians, Goldseekers, and the Rush to Colorado*, calls the central high plains "the roof of the central plains," noting that "no great rivers ran through the rolling swells of land, nearly treeless and covered with short grasses. Outlanders stayed away almost entirely from this region."[4] No wonder—it is a region of extremes: extreme climate, extreme deprivation, and extreme solitude. The first white explorers called the central high plains a desert. Emigrants on their way to the Pacific coast viewed the region with fear, skirting it whenever possible. The central high plains were not country to be settled; they were to be avoided, a region only the truly courageous could love. It was on these central high plains that the Cheyenne made their home.

The Central High Plains

Although the small Cheyenne tribe ranged as far north as the Black Hills of South Dakota and as far south as the Staked Plain of the Texas Panhandle, its camps could generally be found in the plains area between the North Platte and Arkansas Rivers. Eastern Colorado and western Kansas and Nebraska were true Cheyenne country.

The climate in this region was harsh. A winter hunt could prove more dangerous than the most heated of battles. With no trees or natural breaks to block the frigid winds, an exposed hunter caught unexpectedly in a blizzard would have time to do little more than sing his death song. Summer thunderstorms, with hailstones the size of robins' eggs, could bludgeon a war party to death in minutes. Yet there was little water.

The Cheyenne learned to deal with chancy water supplies. A leading Cheyenne authority, E. Adamson Hoebel, notes, "A deficiency of water is in fact the distinguishing climatic characteristic. Most of the precipitation falls in the summer, often in the form of stupendous, crashing thunderstorms. The runoff is quick, except where water gathers in buffalo wallows, and the evaporation rate during the hot, dry days is high."[5] Rivers and streams were undependable: entire sections dried up in late summer and early fall. Those familiar with the country, though, as were the Cheyenne, could usually find water from underground springs and seeps.

With deadly weather, no shelter, and unreliable water sources, one might question the Cheyenne's decision to inhabit this inhospitable area. Yet there were lures that compelled them onto the central plains; one of the strongest was the availability of game. The central high plains were coated with sturdy tufts of buffalo grass, which retained its nutritive values throughout winter's cold and summer's heat. And where there was buffalo grass, there were buffalo.

A Cheyenne settlement on the central high plains, a bare land offering little water and no protection from the often harsh weather.

Although the central high plains were inhospitable to humans, the abundant buffalo grass provided sustenance for the millions of buffalo that once roamed the area.

The American Bison

The shaggy behemoth known as the American bison is the largest of all North American land mammals. It is a relic of prehistoric times and can best be described as magnificently ugly, with its shaggy forequarters, huge hump, and small eyes glaring out from its woolly crown. The central plains boasted buffalo herds numbering in the millions. Early explorers and fur traders wrote of riding for hours, even days, through one herd before reaching its end. According to Berthrong, in the early nineteenth century, "two vast buffalo herds roamed the Plains—one south and one north of the Platte River."[6] The Cheyenne considered the southern herd theirs.

These buffalo satisfied all of the Cheyenne's needs. After a hunt, they feasted on its lungs, liver, tongue, nose, bone marrow, and blood. Its flesh was sliced into strips, dried on tripods in the sun until black, pounded flat, and stored for lean times. The untanned hide, called rawhide, had several uses, including being used to fashion storage containers, saddles, and ropes. Ropes were also made of twisted buffalo hair. Sinews were used for sewing. Bones served as awls, toys, and game pieces.

Most important was the hide. Buffalo hides, along with the horse, formed the basis of the Cheyenne economy. They had no clanking metal coins, no crisp bills with which to purchase goods. Buffalo hides were an important trade item, a source of unlimited wealth for the skilled hunter and his family. The hide also served as clothing and bedding. During the winter the Cheyenne clutched thick russet robes tightly around their shoulders, hair-side in. At winter's severest, with temperatures well below zero, they lay snugly beneath mounds of buffalo robes, rising only to replenish their tepee fires.

Buffalo hides also covered the Cheyenne tepee, or lodge, a conical structure framed with angled poles. When properly constructed, the tepee was warm and dry on bitterly cold days and cool and airy on hot ones. All of the Great Plains tribes used tepees, but the Cheyenne tepees were unique for their immense size and beauty. Moore reports:

> The Cheyennes were noted for having tipis [tepees] that were "white as linen" because they used a tanning process which produced white buffalo skins. This whiteness was enhanced by the application of white clay or of baked selenite, a form of gypsum. When selenite was used, the tipis were not only white, but actually sparkled in the sun.[7]

Hunting Game on the Central Plains

Buffalo are dangerous. They are large animals—a bull can weigh as much as two thousand pounds—and can be nasty, wheeling on their attacker, their horn-studded heads lowered in rage. The Cheyenne used a number of hunting techniques, including ambushes, traps, stalking, and surrounds, to minimize this

Cheyenne tepees were constructed using specially prepared buffalo skins.

15

The Cheyenne Tepee

From the outside, the Cheyenne tepee looks deceptively simple, merely poles angled against one another and draped with a large covering of seamed buffalo hides. Once inside the cone-shaped structure, however, one can only marvel at the ingenuity of the design and the comfort of the living quarters.

Entering the tepee requires a step down. The earthen floor is lowered and the interior has been lined to minimize drafts seeping in at the edges; in especially cold weather, the Cheyenne also stuff dry grass between the lining and the tepee cover for insulation.

Resting on bunches of rye grass, mattresses made of willow branches lie end to end around the lodge. For comfort, the mattresses are covered with mats made of woven rushes, and the mats are covered with layers of buffalo robes. What little wind might squeeze between the tepee cover and the lining rises upward, providing an excellent draft for the central fire.

Between each mattress, at the head of one and the foot of another, is a tripod made of willow branches. A thick buffalo robe drapes over each tripod. Sitting residents can rest their backs against the tripod. As an added bonus, the space beneath each tripod makes a wonderful cabinet for storing containers filled with valuables and winter supplies.

The Cheyenne tepee was intricately designed to keep its occupants cool in summer and warm in winter.

danger. The favorite technique was mounted pursuit, as described by Frank Roe in *The Indian and His Horse:*

> Horse and buffalo raced neck-and-neck, and afforded the rider an unequalled opportunity to plant a fatal arrow or bullet in that most vulnerable spot behind the shoulder, which commonly brought the great beast down, while the well-trained horse jumped aside to avoid being crushed beneath the fallen giant.[8]

Although the buffalo was the Cheyenne's prey of choice, they hunted a wide variety of game. Another favorite was the antelope, a small, incredibly swift relative of the deer. In the eighteenth and early nineteenth centuries, antelope traveled in herds of thousands. They were difficult to pursue on horseback, though, so the Cheyenne devised a unique antelope-hunting method, the antelope pit, to trap the animals.

The hides of deer and elk made soft, pliable clothing, and their flesh was delicious. When traveling in the north, the Cheyenne hunted mountain sheep in the Black Hills and Yellowstone country. Wolves could be caught in baited pit-traps and foxes in deadfall traps. These pelts were especially luxurious, and the meat of the cubs and kits was a delicacy. Badgers and skunks were consumed, but for unknown reasons, otters were taken only for their sleek velveteen furs. Beavers offered silky mahogany hides. Turtles were a prized treat, and fish were easily caught by this tribe with a lake and river heritage.

The Cheyenne savored most waterfowl, but "they eat neither birds of prey nor crows, except under stress of hunger," according to anthropologist George Bird Grinnell, adding: "The magpie they do not eat at all, because, they say, it won for them the race during the contest to see whether the buffalo should eat the people or the people should eat the buffalo."[9]

Gathering the Flora of the Central Great Plains

The Cheyenne's diet included a treasure trove of plants. One species of thistle had a stem tasting like banana. The berries and leaves of red cedar were boiled into a tea. A meal made from pulverized acorns created a tasty mush when boiled with buffalo fat. The sap of the box elder was sweet and, when boiled with hide scrapings, made a wonderful candy for adults and children alike. Fruit from the prickly pear cactus was an esteemed stew ingredient, as were the buds of milkweed.

Fruit abounded. Grinnell lists these as "sarvis-berries, plums, choke-cherries, sand-cherries, bull-berries, and currants."[10] The undisputed favorite of the Cheyenne was the chokecherry. When pounded fine, pits and all, and mixed with dried buffalo meat, chokecherries imparted their tart flavor to the delightful Great Plains staple called pemmican. Chokecherries and other fruits were pounded to a pulp and shaped into small, flat cakes before drying. These Cheyenne fruit cakes were stored for future use in rawhide containers known as parfleches.

The plant most important to the Cheyenne was the Indian turnip. This turnip, high in starch, supplied most of their carbohydrates. It could be eaten raw if young and crunchy. If coarse, it was eaten boiled. The Cheyenne women sliced and dried large quantities of this turnip, storing them for later. The slices could be ground into a soup thickener, akin to modern-day cornstarch, and they were also a valuable trade item.

Harvesting the Indian turnip was a job for women and children. "Children were taught to find the plants by their hairy stems and yellowish-blue flowers," reports West. "Mothers then dug the thick roots and stored them for winter meals."[11] The women harvested in groups, using a sacred tool called a dibble. The typical dibble was long and made of wood with one sharp end. This end was thrust into the soil beneath the turnip and then levered upward, bringing the precious tuber with it.

Cheyenne women were proud of their tools, often passing them on to their daughters. In addition to the dibble, there was the stone maul, an indispensable tool for pulverizing meat, fruit, and vegetables. Hide preparation required four tools: a

Cheyenne women prepare food for a feast. The Cheyenne's diet was varied and included buffalo meat, Indian turnips, and chokecherries.

The Cheyenne formed large camps and moved every few days. It was the women's duty to dismantle, pack, move, and reconstruct the tepees with every move.

stone scraper to remove flesh and fat, an elk-horn flesher to thin the skin to an even thickness, a buffalo shoulder blade to pull the hide through during the softening process, and a willow draw-blade to remove the hair if desired.

Cheyenne Camps

Camps were large. The more hunters, the more successful the hunt. Because many people made for countless horses, however, forage was quickly depleted, so the

Cheyenne broke camp every few days. Scouts were sent into the surrounding territory, seeking a location choked with buffalo grass and buffalo. Upon their return, the women dismantled their tepees, folding the tepee cover and attaching the poles to horses and dogs. Binding the ends with several evenly spaced rawhide thongs, they created a travois, a platform on which they piled their parfleches filled with meat, turnips, and fruit cakes. Urging the horses and dogs forward, they followed

Winter Camps

Colonel Richard I. Dodge, stationed in Southern Cheyenne territory for much of his career with the U.S. military, enjoyed observing Great Plains life. Below, in an excerpt from his book *Our Wild Indians*, he describes a typical Plains Indian winter camp.

"To Indians at peace, and with food in plenty, the winter camp is the scene of constant enjoyment. After the varying excitements, the successes and vicissitudes, the constant labors of many months, the prospect of the winter's peace and rest, with its home life and home pleasures, comes like a soothing balm to all.

To . . . [old men], this season brings the full enjoyment of those pleasures and excitement left to them in life. Their days are spent in gambling, their long winter evenings in endless repetitions of stories of their wonderful performances in days gone by, and their nights in the sound sweet sleep vouchsafed [granted] only to easy consciences.

The old women also have a good time. No more taking down and putting up the tepee, no more packing and unpacking the ponies. To bring the wood and water, do the little cooking, to attend to the ponies, and possibly to dress a few skins, is all the labor devolved on them.

To the young of both sexes, whether married or single, this season brings unending excitement and pleasure. Now is the time for dances and feasts, for visits and frolics, and merry-makings of all kinds. . . . "

their men to the new campsite, where they erected the tepees. This process was repeated again and again until the days shortened.

Winters were spent in a sheltered place, someplace with enough timber to feed the tepee fires and to keep the wind at bay. A favorite location was along the Arkansas River in present-day Kansas. Lewis H. Garrard, who in 1846 as a seventeen-year-old with a serious case of wanderlust stayed with the Cheyenne, writes, "This particular vicinity is called the 'Big Timber'—a strip of woods extending for several miles along the river. As a general thing, there is little or no timber on the Arkansas from the Cimmarone crossing to the headwaters, with the exception of this belt, which the Indians consider their future home."[12] Stretches of timber were rare, but the Cheyenne knew them all, heading for their favorites when the frost began to wither the grass.

Winter camps were semipermanent. With knee-high snow and a fickle climate, the Cheyenne lacked mobility during this season and moved only under duress. It did not take many horses to denude the ground, so their winter camps—called a vestoz—were small, composed of only a few dozen people. Even so, the horses suffered. Pawing beneath the crusted snow, the animals were rewarded only with snatches of frozen grass.

As spring returned, the horses fattened quickly on the early buffalo grass. When winter camps broke, the Cheyenne returned to the central high plains, overjoyed at having completed another central high plains seasonal cycle.

Chapter 2

Social and Religious Customs

Anthropologists maintain that the hallmark of civilization is the presence of a written language, which the Cheyenne lacked in their early days. Yet the Cheyenne were in many ways as civilized as the Europeans who settled their land. Cheyenne expert Stan Hoig qualifies this as a presettlement state, saying:

> During the early years of western exploration, before contamination of Indian life by the white man's diseases and whisky, the Cheyennes were recognized as having one of the highest Indian cultures on the plains. White explorers considered the Cheyenne mode of living to be cleaner, their women more chaste, and their sense of personal dignity stronger than most other tribes.[13]

Homicide of Cheyenne by Cheyenne was rare. Child abuse was not tolerated. Generosity, courage, respect for elders, cleanliness—these are only a few of the virtues lauded by Cheyenne society.

The Cheyenne, widely scattered across an area as large as England, were unified by their customs. All adhered to the same

Portrait of a young Cheyenne woman.

social standards and legal codes; all worshiped the same god and revered the same cultural heroes. Those reluctant to accept these laws, standards, and beliefs were shunned or exiled. The opinions and company of their peers were important to all Cheyenne. Few courted the displeasure of the elders. As a result, the Cheyenne achieved a uniformity of civilization.

Appearance and Dress

The Cheyenne were uniformly attractive. Western author and artist Frederic Remington counted Cheyenne women among the most beautiful Native Americans he met, noting, "Indeed, some of them are quite as I imagine Pocahontas, Minnehaha, and the rest of the heroines of the race appeared."[14] Missionary Pierre-Jean de Smet had similar praise for the men he met in 1840, commenting on their facial features, height, and strength. Appearance was important to the Cheyenne. From accessories to makeup, grooming to apparel, both genders exercised detailed diligence.

In early times, the men wore nose rings made of shells strung on a rawhide thong. When the first white traders appeared, bringing colorful glass beads and shiny metals, nose rings gave way to earrings. The outer edge of the ears was slit and wrapped with beaded strings. The men also liked flattened coins, which they bound to a braid of buffalo hair before fas-

Cheyenne men groomed themselves carefully and wore extensive accessories.

tening them to their own locks. Brass bracelets became fashionable among the women. Both genders painted their faces, and it was a sign of deep affection for a Cheyenne man to paint his wife's face in scarlet hues.

They were renowned for their hair length—the hair of some Cheyenne men touched the ground when freed from its braids. Women bundled thick braids behind their ears, wrapping them in deerskin before painting the tops of their heads with red streaks. The Cheyenne combed their hair with dried buffalo tongues or porcupine tails to keep it glossy and tangle-free. The men groomed themselves with special care, according to Grinnell, who writes, "Some young men devoted much time to their personal appearance, plucking out the hairs from eyebrows, lips, and cheeks, combing and braiding their hair, and painting their faces."[15]

Casual clothes for the men consisted of a breechcloth, leggings, and moccasins when it was warm. They wore buffalo robes when it was cold. For more formal occasions, the leggings and moccasins were decorated with brightly dyed porcupine quills and reeds. The leggings were fringed with strips of buckskin, and the buffalo robe painted and exquisitely ornamented. A quilled, satiny buckskin tunic was also worn, and tunics of successful warriors might be fringed with the hair of their enemies.

Cheyenne women wore a simply cut dress of soft buckskin, flowing in an unbro-

Quilling

Cheyenne women took great pride in their quillwork, which was a laborious process. First a design was created, sketched in the dust or snow with a stick, perhaps obliterated many times and redrawn until it was exactly right. Colors were chosen with an eye to beauty, contrast, and appropriateness to design. Next the stiff, barbed porcupine quills were soaked in dye-laced water until they emerged soft and brilliantly colored. Hands were coated with white clay or gypsum to prevent them from staining the leather with natural oils. Using buffalo sinew that had been separated again and again until incredibly fine, the women attached the quills to the plain leather, inserting the sinew at the back of the quill, where it would not show. Occasionally a woman would pause to slide a buffalo shoulder blade over the quills,

smoothing them down. Attaching one quill at a time to a garment designed to bear hundreds, even thousands, was a labor of tremendous love.

The women liked to work in company, in what were called quilling societies. These groups were a type of artists guild. The more experience a woman had quilling, the higher within the guild she would rise, until she reached the enviable position of instructor, with her services available to those willing to pay her price. Novices began with moccasins, working their way up through baby cradles, lodge star ornaments, buffalo robes, lodge linings, backrests, and parfleches. Any woman having quilled thirty robes or having tackled the daunting task of ornamenting an entire lodge by herself was revered within the tribe.

A Southern Cheyenne family outside their home.

ken line from neck to midcalf. Their legs and feet were clad in form-fitting leggings and moccasins. Formal dresses were vividly decorated with quills, reeds, shells, beads, and elk's teeth. Elk's teeth were prized and rare, and a Cheyenne man could gain preference with a woman by giving her a thick packet of elk's teeth. And gaining preference was important, given the value the Cheyenne men placed on marriage.

Gender Roles

Securing a good wife was a grave matter to Cheyenne men. An industrious wife made a comfortable home. In *Our Wild Indians*, Colonel Richard I. Dodge lists the duties of a good wife as follows:

The pride of a good wife is in permitting her husband to do nothing for himself. She cooks his food, makes and mends his lodge and his clothing, dresses skins, butchers the game, dries the meat, goes after and saddles his horse.

When making a journey she strikes the lodge, packs the animals, cares for all the babies, and superintends the march, her lord and master, who left camp long before her, being far off in the front or flank looking after game.

On arriving at the camping place, she unpacks the animals, pitches the lodge, makes the beds, brings wood and water, and does everything that is to be done, and when her husband returns from his hunt, is ready to take and unsaddle his horse.[16]

Brave Men Only Need Apply

John Stands in Timber, a Northern Cheyenne, devoted his life to studying the history and customs of his ancestors. With the help of Cheyenne expert Margot Liberty, he was able to document his findings in *Cheyenne Memories*. The following excerpt from that book partially explains the courage of Cheyenne men in battle.

"A man could not even court a girl unless he had proved his courage. That was one reason so many were anxious to win good war records. A girl's mother was with her all the time, and if he walked up to her the mother would talk about him and ask what he had done in battle. In fact they were all afraid of what people, and especially the women, would say if they were cowardly. The women even had a song they would sing about a man whose courage had failed him. The song was: 'If you are afraid when you charge, turn back. The Desert Women will eat you.' It meant the women would talk about him so badly it would have been better to die. And they had another song: 'If you had fought bravely I would have sung for you.' It meant the same thing. My grandfather and others used to tell me that hearing the women sing that way made them ready to do anything. It was hard to go into a fight, and they were often afraid, but it was worse to turn back and face the women. It was one reason they didn't show being scared, but went right in; they were forced to."

Cheyenne men also esteemed sweetness, generosity, and modesty. Of primary importance, though, was chastity. From an early age, Cheyenne women wore a chastity belt, a rope looped about the waist, run between the legs, and tied around their thighs.

Cheyenne women sought courage and skill in their men. A good husband defended his family with his life. He was the first to ride into battle and the last to leave. His arrows and bullets always found their target. He was a good provider. When game became scarce in winter, he was unafraid to brave the deadly plains. Cheyenne women were hard on their men, loudly mocking those who failed to demonstrate courage. One Cheyenne elder, explaining the renowned Cheyenne bravery in battle, said most warriors feared the taunts of their women more than they feared death.

Courtship and Marriage

This courage, however, was notably lacking in courtship. Having found the right woman, the young Cheyenne man became shy around her, taking as long as six years to propose marriage. According to Hoebel,

Once a boy has seen a girl whom he hopes to make his sweetheart, he approaches her furtively. He knows the path from her family lodge to the stream where she gets water or the grove where she gathers wood. Hopefully, he stands along the path. As she passes, he gives her robe a little tug. Perhaps he feels this is too bold. If so, he whistles or calls to her. She may stonily ignore him, much to his mortification. Or she may make the stars shine by stopping to talk about this or that, but never of love. If all goes well, they may later begin to meet and talk outside her lodge.[17]

The Cheyenne had an interesting attitude toward marriage and courtship. Although they greatly valued marriage, divorce was not out of the question. The families arranged all marriages, which was no guarantee the marriage would be lasting. Marriage with a member of friendly tribes was encouraged if the newlyweds planned to live with the Cheyenne. The Cheyenne's numbers were few and those of their enemies many. To retain their position, the Cheyenne needed to maintain their population.

Above all else, Cheyenne women valued bravery in their men.

Children and Child Rearing

It was hoped that new marriages would soon be blessed with children. Life on the central plains was brutal. Women bore only a few children, and many children did not survive infancy. The birth of a child was a grand occasion, and the Cheyenne had a number of interesting child-rearing techniques.

Their legendary patience was one. When a young child cried in anger or frustration, he or she was ignored. If the behavior occurred in the presence of elders, the mother placed the child in a cradleboard, which she deposited at a distant location until the disruptive wails tapered to whimpers. Garrard speaks amusingly of one young boy, Jack Smith, son of a fur trader and his Cheyenne wife. Jack was a terror. At the slightest provocation, he inflated his lungs and erupted with a series of ear-splitting howls. Other than glaring at her husband, the wife did not react to the noise at all.

Striking a child, especially young boys, was considered reprehensible. Young boys would not mature into courageous men if made timid. As Garrard explains, "The Indians never chastise a boy, as they think his spirit would be broken and *cowed* down, and instead of a warrior, he would be a *squaw*—a harsh epithet, indicative of cowardice—and they resort to any method but infliction of blows to subdue a refractory scion."[18]

Early on, boys learned their roles as warriors and hunters. They were given miniature weapons as toys and taught to use them well. From the day they could straddle a pony's back, they became tiny equestrians.

Although the girls were also taught to ride, their primary role was to keep house. They were allowed to play with their brothers until young adults, and many enjoyable hours were spent playing Indian village. The girls kept little tepees while their brothers fought off mock

The birth of a child was a major event for the Cheyenne.

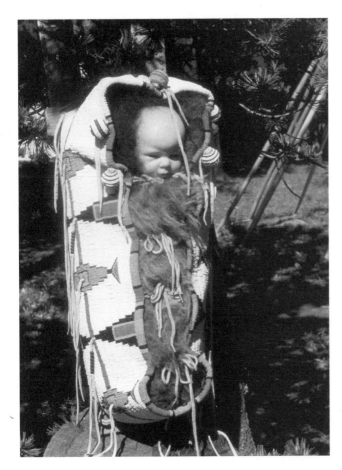

A Cheyenne baby rests snugly in an intricately decorated cradleboard.

enemies and killed small game with their miniature arrows.

Mourning and Burial Customs

The courageous Cheyenne men often died in battle. When this happened, their women loudly mourned them. Slitting the flesh on their forehead, arms, and legs with a sharp knife, they cried while wandering about the camp, long hair shorn, bare skin gleaming beneath a slick coating of blood. This mourning custom was more than a method of honoring the dead. It was also a means of coercing the living warriors to avenge his death.

The dead were buried at a location far from camp. The Cheyenne buried their dead with some possessions. A warrior's horses might be shot, and his bow and arrows placed at his side. A dead woman rested beside her tools. Shields, war bonnets, and fleshers, however, were considered heirlooms and generally passed on to the living. The Cheyenne also dressed and painted the body before placing it high on a platform, either in a tree or on a scaffold. "It must be a sound, strong tree," explains Dodge, "well sheltered, and apparently safe from any chance of being uprooted by the terrific wind-storms of the Plains. The branches must be so situated that the final resting place will be nearly horizontal."[19]

In later years, consideration was given to finding a tree far from white settlements and trails. Many of the emigrants, fascinated by the Cheyenne grave sites, plucked souvenirs from the corpses. Without these possessions, the Cheyenne believed they were doomed to an immaterial afterlife.

Cheyenne Religion and Cultural Heroes

These possessions were used in the Cheyenne version of heaven. There the dead lived in harmony with Maheo, the creator of the world and everything in it. Four Sacred Persons, the Maheyuno, were positioned at the four directions of the compass, where they guarded Maheo's creation. "Sometimes," writes Father Peter Powell in *Sweet Medicine*, "they appear in visions as men on horseback."[20] The Maheyuno controlled the Maiyun, lesser spirits who appeared to men in a variety of forms, such as animals or birds. The Cheyenne worshiped their deity, Maheo, by dancing, performing elaborate ceremonies and rituals, and offering him the smoke from their pipes.

The Cheyenne also had two cultural heroes: Sweet Medicine and Erect Horns. These cultural heroes, who were legendary persons—and, as such, evidence of their actual existence is undetermined—were responsible for giving the Cheyenne their laws and the vital necessities of buffalo and corn. In them, the Cheyenne found something to believe in.

According to Cheyenne legend, Sweet Medicine was born to a young unmarried woman. Abandoned at birth, he was raised by an old childless woman. Sweet Medicine was a strange boy who possessed powerful medicine, or holy power. The elders of the tribe thought him too arrogant. After violently tussling with an elder over a buffalo hide, he was exiled from the tribe and disappeared for four years. When

Mahuts

Anthropologist George H. Dorsey is one of only a handful of white men to have seen the Cheyenne sacred arrows. In an excerpt from *The Cheyenne*, he depicts them as follows:

"They are about thirty-inches long, one-half an inch in diameter, round, very straight, with flint stone points. The points are tied in at the end, and over each of the four arrow points is tied a covering of white, downy eagle feathers. At the other end are whole wing feathers of the eagle,

split in two, and tied on each side of the arrows. The shafts are also partly covered with the white, downy feathers of an eagle. All the feathers are painted red. On each of the four arrows are painted figures of the world, the blue paint meaning blue heavens, the sun, moon, stars, the red paint meaning the earth. Buffalo and other animals are also painted. So these sacred arrows are held symbolic of the Great Medicine [Maheo], who made the sun, moon, and the stars, and the earth."

Sweet Medicine returned, he told of having visited the Black Hills in South Dakota. There, in the sacred mountain called Nowah'wus, he met several elders, who gave him laws, as well as buffalo and corn. Their most important gift, however, was four sacred arrows, the Mahuts: two man-arrows and two buffalo-arrows, which the Cheyenne believed held magic powers that would help them in battle and the hunt.

The story of Erect Horns is similar in some aspects. He also visited a sacred mountain where he received instruction and gifts from sacred elders. He was taught the Medicine Lodge ceremony, which the Cheyenne used to celebrate their national unity. In addition to buffalo and corn, Erect Horns was given the sacred buffalo hat, or Is'siwun. Berthrong says of Is'siwun, "If properly respected, the buffalo hat brought abundant food, good health, and adequate clothing and shelter to the Cheyenne."[21]

The Sweet Medicine legend explains the tribe's organization and its success as warriors and hunters. Erect Horns' instructions and gifts were an assurance of fertility and plentitude. Between Sweet Medicine and Erect Horns, the Cheyenne became a powerful tribe. Is'siwun ensured fertility and wealth; Mahuts, success in war and the hunt.

The standards of behavior for each individual Cheyenne were exacting. These standards, a product of their beliefs in Maheo and their two cultural heroes, helped create a uniform civilization not present in some other Great Plains tribes.

Chapter 3

War and Peace: Peace Chiefs and War Leaders

There was a decided distinction between the behaviors of Cheyenne at peace and Cheyenne at war. On the one hand, they were civilized to a high degree, a dignified people with a rigid legal code. On the other hand, they fought with savagery. When

A white hunter lies dead on the ground, the victim of a Cheyenne scalping.

dealing with enemies, the Cheyenne did not hesitate to take scalps, sometimes while the victim was still alive; to mutilate enemy corpses, perhaps collecting fingers for a gruesome necklace; or to dishonor captive women. They were dervishes in battle, howling as they raced their horses through enemy lines.

The reason for this contradiction lies in the Cheyenne government, given in ancient times by Sweet Medicine. Cheyenne historian John Stands in Timber, speaking of the prophet's visit to Nowah'wus, writes, "Sweet Medicine learned next that he was to give the people a good government, with forty-four chiefs to manage it, and a good system of police and military protection. . . ."[22] Therefore, the Cheyenne had chiefs for peace and leaders for war. The peace chiefs and war leaders, as they were called, enforced the unwritten code of behavior by which all Cheyenne lived.

Peace Chiefs and the Council of Forty-four

The peace chiefs met each year as the Council of Forty-four. The council, consisting of four supreme chiefs representing all members of the Cheyenne Nation and forty others selected from the ten Cheyenne bands, decided important issues such as when and where to hunt and move. Every ten years, most of the council resigned, and a new group was elected. Each outgoing chief suggested a candidate for his vacancy. Because many advocated their sons or the sons of other peace chiefs, the job was often, but not necessarily, hereditary.

The duties of a peace chief were strenuous. In addition to his council duties, his behavior and attitude had to be exemplary. According to West, peace chiefs "were selected for their sagacity, courage, generosity, and self-control."[23] A good peace chief had to possess wisdom beyond the average. He was a priest, skilled in the rituals of the Cheyenne religion. He must have demonstrated extraordinary bravery. Many of the peace chiefs had been war leaders in their youth; all had been warriors. He had to be generous. An often-told story concerns one peace chief who, encountering an impoverished Arapaho, dismounted his horse and gave it to the poor man. Other stories tell of peace chiefs who, when asked to lend an item to a tribesman, gave it to him outright. Self-control, however, was the peace chief's most important attribute. According to Hoebel, "Chiefs . . . sometimes show

Cheyenne peace chiefs like this one gathered annually as the Council of Forty-four.

their superiority to . . . indignity by remarking most casually, 'A dog has [urinated] on my tipi.'"[24]

The practice of these virtues gave the peace chiefs extraordinary influence over their bands and the tribe. However, they were reluctant to make final decisions regarding war. That authority rested with the Cheyenne war societies and their leaders. Hoig explains this division of duties, saying, "A chief's authority was primarily a moral authority, subject to the respect accorded him by the people. . . . [I]t was the war societies who controlled the fighting men and led them into battle . . . keeping the peace within and without the tribe was the chief's principal responsibility."[25] When war appeared imminent, the prudent peace chiefs turned to the war societies.

Warrior Societies and War Leaders

The war societies, also called fraternities, were responsible for defense and for avenging deaths. They also enforced the law. Whenever the peace chiefs decided to move the camp, they appointed one of the war societies to direct the movement. The society spurred on laggards and monitored the wayward. Another society would be chosen to police the hunt, making certain no single hunter violated policy by shooting before everyone was in position. Sweet Medicine gave the Cheyenne four of these societies; in later years there were as many as seven: Bow-

string Soldiers, Wolf Soldiers, Crazy Dogs, Red Shields, Dog Soldiers, Kit Foxes, and Elk Soldiers. Each society was governed by major and minor leaders, warriors who exemplified courage, skill, and daring.

By the age of fifteen or sixteen, most Cheyenne boys joined a fraternity. When determining which group to join, a young man often chose his father's society. He began as an ordinary member, dressing and dancing in the manner unique to his society and fighting in its ranks.

If a boy distinguished himself in battle, he might be elected to a four-year term as a minor leader. Each fraternity had several minor leaders, men who led the ranks into battle. Being elected a minor war leader was an honor. A Cheyenne man might wear a special emblem or shirt proclaiming his new position. At fraternity dances, he might be entitled to sing a special song indicative of his office.

Being a minor leader was also a big responsibility. His behavior in and around the camp was subject to the scrutiny of tribal members. Elders watched how he behaved with others, paying special attention to how he handled himself when angry. Because the Cheyenne valued patience and control, demonstrations of anger or violence were strongly discouraged. A good minor leader never lost his temper and always maintained his composure.

When electing the major war leaders, great leaders whose names were remem-

Fraternities and Women

Women were not allowed to join the warrior societies, with one exception. Donald J. Berthrong, author of *The Southern Cheyennes*, explains:

"Three of the warrior societies admitted four maidens as associates into their organizations. From prominent families, preferably those of chiefs, the young women had duties confined to the society's ceremonial functions. They participated in the soldiers' dances, were present at the feasts, and sat in front of the war chiefs in all the councils. Sweet Medicine gave the soldier societies the privilege of allowing four maidens in their association but required that they be 'chaste and clean.'"

The Dog Soldiers and the Bowstrings, however, were adamant that no women be admitted. An unchaste woman associate could result in disas-

In pre-reservation times, the big chief was flatly "selected to die." That is, he was supposed to be so fearless and aggressive in battle that he would not survive his term of office. Typically, a warrior "selected to die" would give away most or all of his possessions, and might give up buffalo hunting and social activities to devote himself entirely to war medicines, prayer, and fasting. During this time he would be supported by family members and society members, who would bring him and his family food, clothing, and other necessities. Men who took "the war road," that is, men who aspired to be war leaders, frequently eschewed [avoided] marriage and family and became loners, living with a parent, brother, sister or friend.[26]

The war leaders had three primary duties. First, they planned the battle. Second, they were first to engage the enemy, riding at the head of their men. Third, if the battle went poorly for the Cheyenne, the war leaders rallied their troops by fighting with reckless abandon, frequently to the death.

The Dog Soldiers

When the Cheyenne waged war against other tribes or the United States government, the societies generally joined forces. The one exception, however, was the Dog Soldiers. In the early part of the nineteenth century, a war leader of this fraternity

bered long after their deaths, each society drew upon its pool of minor leaders. Depending on the fraternity, there were between one and four war leaders who served a four-year term. It was these war leaders who wrote Cheyenne history, often with their own blood. Moore, who calls these distinguished warriors "big chiefs," describes their duties as follows:

A Cheyenne warrior poses in the traditional dress of his war society.

Council of Forty-four and, as a result, according to Berthrong, "were not governed by the usual band chiefs but by their own military chiefs."[27] Without peace chiefs to balance their war leaders, the Dog Soldiers spent much of their time at war. They did not tolerate interlopers and were quick to avenge the death of any member of the Cheyenne Nation, regardless of band affiliation. It is the Dog Soldiers who are credited with earning the Cheyenne their reputation as hostile, unrelenting warriors.

The Psychology of War

Although all Cheyenne war societies used psychological tactics, the Dog Soldiers were famous for theirs. One of their most common war tactics was to send band members into battle wearing a dog rope. This buffalo-skin sash had a small wooden pin fastened at one end, and, according to half-Cheyenne George Bent,

committed that most heinous of Cheyenne crimes, murdering another Cheyenne. He and the members of his society were exiled. These fierce warriors took their wives and children with them and formed their own band. The Dog Soldiers existed on their own and formed strong ties within their group. They did not participate in the

when caught in a desperate situation, the wearer of the dog rope dismounted and drove the picket pin into the ground. Here he must remain. Should the fight go against the party he would be disgraced if he pulled up the pin and retreated. However, another warrior could release him by pulling the picket pin and driving the wearer of the dog rope off the field by striking him a few times with a quirt. The idea was that the wearer of the sash was so brave that he would not retreat after staking himself to the ground and that the man who released him had to whip him like a dog to compel him to retreat.[28]

The advantages of this practice were twofold. It served to rally the staked man's comrades, who were sworn to die protecting one another. It also tended to put a damper on the valor of the enemy. Those who had fought the Cheyenne before surely quaked at the sight of a dog rope being staked to the ground. They knew what this action meant—the Dog Soldiers would now fight with frenzy.

Other war societies used similar tactics. One was the practice of counting coup. When a slain enemy fell in battle, his Cheyenne assailant did not receive any distinction other than that of being an accurate shot. Distinction was reserved for the first few men to touch the body, or "count coup" upon it. Some warriors touched it with a weapon or bare hand; others used a short painted stick. According to Dodge, "In a fight, when an enemy falls, all those warriors in the vicinity rush for the body, each exerting every effort to be the first to strike it, those in the rear hurling their 'coup-sticks' at long distances in the hope of a fortunate strike."[29] The sight of these massed warriors swiftly advancing often intimidated the enemy and could turn a battle in the Cheyenne's favor.

Battle Tactics

Sometimes the Cheyenne utilized battle tactics that were not so much psychological in nature but simply founded on good warfare strategy. One of their favorites was the ambush. The central plains are seamed with ravines, erosive splits in rocky areas that cannot be seen from most angles. Suspecting that an enemy's path would cross near one of these ravines, the Cheyenne warriors concealed themselves in its depths. They and their horses rested in the cool shade while their enemy labored toward them through the hot sun. When the enemy passed, the warriors exploded from the ravine on fresh horses, quickly dispatching their foe.

Another favorite tactic was to send a small party of warriors across the path of an advancing enemy party, not so close that they could be shot, but close enough that the foes could see them. Pretending surprise at the enemy's presence, the Cheyenne warriors urged their ponies away at a smart pace, leading their unwary pursuers on a chase across the plains. Nearer and nearer the enemy drew. Arrows began to fly. Blood running high, perhaps chuckling at the thought of an easy victory over the hapless Cheyenne, the interlopers rounded a corner at reckless speed and then slid their mounts to a dust-boiling halt at the sight of hundreds of armed Cheyenne warriors.

Religion and War

Religion also played a major role in Cheyenne psychological warfare. When the Cheyenne tribe declared war against another tribe, all the bands gathered in one huge camp before moving. Warriors joined their fraternity battalions; women and children packed their homes and possessions on travois. At the front of this massive army rode the Keeper of the Hat, the horned Is'siwun upon his head. Beside him rode the Keeper of the Arrows, with Mahuts lashed to a lance pointed in the direction of the enemy forces. The warriors were always spiritually empowered by the sight of the sacred arrows before them. In fact, Powell writes that of the six recorded times the Mahuts were used against an enemy in this manner, "in three cases, Cheyenne warriors, eager to count the first coups, charged before the blinding ceremonies could be completed. Thus they neutralized the power of Mahuts."[30] In all three cases, the Cheyenne lost the battle.

Religious beliefs were also important to the individual. Each warrior had his own personal medicine (power), communicated to him by Maheo in the form of visions, dreams, and events. Following a priest's instructions, a warrior prepared himself for battle by applying paint and dressing in the prescribed manner. The Cheyenne believed a war bonnet made by a priest and ceremonially blessed could be especially potent in repelling bullets. The same

An illustration called "White Hunter," from a Cheyenne ledger, shows a Cheyenne warrior charging his enemy wielding a shield and lance.

Suicide Boys

Sometimes a young man decided that life was too harsh, that he no longer wanted to live. Although suicide was generally against Cheyenne law, suicide in battle was esteemed. For this reason, a world-weary boy might vow to take his life in the next battle. Regarding suicide boys, John H. Moore, Cheyenne anthropologist and historian, quotes a Bowstring Soldier in the following excerpt from *The Cheyenne*.

"If there were some suicide boys who had made a vow, they were allowed to start the battle. They went to the front to fulfill their vow. They had no medicine [power] to protect themselves. They were naked, and there was nothing on their bodies or their horses that the enemy could take as loot. They gave their bodies to the enemy for different reasons, maybe to honor someone, or to take revenge, or because they had a dream or because they were sick or unhappy or tired of living, or because some girl had turned them down—different reasons. But they all knew that when they started fighting, no one would help them. The other warriors all honored their suicide vows, and tried to help them die honorably. The warriors shouted encouragement to the suicide boys as they attacked the enemy, naked and without weapons.

The suicide boys would trot their horses toward the enemy and sing their death songs. . . . And then the Cheyenne warriors all yelled and the suicide boys charged among the enemy, hitting them with their fists, pulling them off their horses, choking them and biting them until the enemy gathered around them and at last all the suicide boys were dead. That is when things got more serious."

applied to war shirts. A warrior who genuinely believed he was immune to injury would fight without a care, much to the consternation of his foe.

Weapons

When they went to battle, Cheyenne warriors took with them several different weapons. The most sacred was the war shield. Made of dried buffalo-bull hide, the Cheyenne shield was capable of withstanding arrows, lances, and even bullets when fired from a distance. However, the spiritual power of a shield was its most important characteristic. According to Grinnell,

It might exercise in behalf of him who carried it not only the general protective influence due to its sacred character, but also might endue him with those qualities attributed to the heavenly bodies, birds, mammals, and other living creatures whose images were painted on it, or portions of which

A Cheyenne warrior holds a rifle as he scans the horizon.

unavailable or stealth was required, they fought with these.

Bows were made of strong, supple juniper wood or elk antlers that had been soaked until pliable and reshaped. Elastic buffalo sinew served as a bowstring. Cherry bush provided the wood for most shafts, and the arrowheads were made of razor-sharp iron. To make the arrows fly true, the feathers of turkeys or buzzards were preferred since eagle and hawk feathers tended to absorb blood, requiring replacement after each use.

Arrow making was a learned skill. Arrows were made in identical lots of ten. A young man might apprentice to an arrow maker, learning the materials, procedure, and rituals involved. Once his own arrows had been used successfully in battle, he would have all the business he could handle. The Cheyenne were renowned for the accuracy of their arrows. Members of other tribes traveled long distances to trade for arrows from a reputable Cheyenne arrow maker.

The fierce Cheyenne used weapons and psychological tactics to outsmart and outmaneuver their enemies, making the war societies dominant on the battlefield. In times of peace, however, the Cheyenne looked to their chiefs for guidance and direction. These two groups governed the Cheyenne successfully for many years, creating a balance that allowed the nation to survive.

were tied to it. It might afford also protection from the elements, for some shields were sacred to the thunder and to the lightning.[31]

The shield was a defensive weapon, designed to protect. When they launched an offensive attack, however, the Cheyenne, who mostly fought from horseback, used three primary weapons: the gun, the lance, and the bow and arrow. Guns were a wonderful thing to have, but only if the warrior also had ammunition. The lance was difficult to manipulate in a pitched equestrian battle and generally served as a ceremonial weapon particular to each warrior society. Without a doubt, the bow and arrow was the Cheyenne's most prized weapon. When ammunition was

Chapter 4

Trade and Traders

Many factors including timing and location affected Cheyenne trade, but none had more of an influence than the law of supply and demand. A low supply generates a high demand, and Moore notes that "the demands for both robes and horses were increasing at the time the Cheyennes entered the plains."[32] Because the Cheyenne had access to large supplies of these two items, they became a formidable presence in Great Plains trading. They traded with Ute and Paiute to the west, Comanche and Kiowa to the south, Mandan and Arikara to the north, and the Europeans and Americans to the east.

Robes and Horses for Trade

Buffalo robes were in high demand among tribes lacking access to their source, the buffalo herds. They were also a valuable commodity in the eastern United States and Europe, thanks to the decline of beaver in the early nineteenth century. The Cheyenne had a reputation for the high quality of their robes, which further increased the demand. Hide preparation was a back-breaking, time-consuming task, but the Cheyenne women were hard workers and took great pride in the finished product. An industrious woman could prepare two to three dozen robes during winter camp.

Cheyenne women dry meat and prepare buffalo robes in this 1869 drawing.

Another lucrative trade item was the horse. Location was everything when trading horses. A horse was worth little in the south, where the animals were easily had. However, those willing to travel far to the north could realize a good profit on horses. The Cheyenne were barely mounted themselves when they began making the long trek south. Sometimes they stopped to capture horses along the way, dipping into the wild herds scattered across the Great Plains. After roping a fractious mustang, they tied its head to the tail of a gentle mare. By the time they completed their journey, the wild horse was well on its way to being gentled. The Cheyenne were also notorious horsethieves. In 1804 explorer Meriwether Lewis noted in his journal that the Cheyenne "steel [*sic*] horses from the Spanish Settlements, to the S.W. this excurtion [*sic*] they make in one month."[33]

Cheyenne Horse Thieves

In *Our Wild Indians*, Colonel Richard I. Dodge called the Cheyenne the most cunning horse thieves of all Native Americans, writing, "For dash and boldness in thieving, I think the Southern Cheyennes [are the best]. . . ."

According to Dodge, for example, one night a group of soldiers were camped in Cheyenne territory. They knew the Cheyenne were after their horses, so they picketed and hobbled all the mounts (tied up the horses). Night had barely fallen when a huge fireball came rocketing through the camp making a horrible sound. The soldiers quickly fired into the blackness, where they knew the Cheyenne waited. However, some of their terrified horses burst their picket lines and, hobbled as they were, bolted into the night, straight into the waiting arms of the Cheyenne. The next morning the soldiers found a charred Indian pony laying dead at the edge of the camp. The Cheyenne had tied bundles of grass around its barrel (midsection) and neck and, igniting the grass, pointed the pony's head toward the soldier camp.

The Comanche and Kiowa suffered the most at the Cheyenne's sticky hands. Their enormous herds made for easy pickings. A Cheyenne horse-raiding party generally went on foot, with warriors carrying their saddles, bridles, and ropes. Upon arrival at the edge of a Comanche or Kiowa herd, the Cheyenne caught several loose horses, tacking them up in the dead of night. Driving the stolen horses before them, they raced back toward their own camp. Sometimes they were even more daring. Knowing the Comanche kept their best horses picketed by their tepees at night, the Cheyenne made a mad dash on the enemy camp, slashing picket lines and galloping away with the best of the Comanche mounts.

Legendary Cheyenne hero Sweet Medicine prophesied the arrival of white settlers and added that they would eventually dominate Cheyenne land.

Trade was another means of obtaining horses. In the south they used British goods acquired from the Mandan and Arikara to trade with the southern Comanche and Kiowa, who had more horses than they needed. The early-nineteenth-century trading relations proved to be profitable to the Cheyenne. When the Mandan and Arikara were decimated by smallpox in 1837, however, trade suffered and was no longer profitable. Then, at a time when Cheyenne trade desperately needed a boost, another source appeared on the horizon. The Americans arrived in Cheyenne territory.

The Coming of the Americans

Shortly before he died, Sweet Medicine called his people to him and prophesied the coming of the white man, saying, in the words of Powell, "Soon you will find among you a people with hair all over their faces. Their skin will be white. When that time comes, they will control you. The white people will be all over the land, and at last you will disappear."[34] The Cheyenne listened, nodding somberly when the prophet finished. Long after his death, they remembered his words. When Clark, one of the first

Americans encountered by the Cheyenne, offered one peace chief a peace medal in 1806, the chief started backward, refusing it. He told Clark that white men were bad luck. Despite the Indian's fears, Clark talked him into accepting the medal.

Three decades later the peace chief Yellow Wolf did more than accept a medal. He encouraged a fur trader, William Bent, to establish a trading post near the Cheyenne. Bent agreed. In 1834 he and his partners built a sturdy fort on the Arkansas River,

near Big Timbers. Bent's Fort became a busy hub of trade. George Bent, William's son with a Cheyenne woman, describes the trade at Bent's Fort as follows:

Besides trading with the Indians, my father used to send some of his best traders down to New Mexico—to Santa Fe and Taos—with wagonloads of goods from the fort. They brought back from New Mexico horses, mules, cattle, Mexican blankets, silver dollars, and silver bullion in bars. I remember when a boy seeing the wagons come in with their loads of bright colored blankets. The Indians prized these blankets with their stripes of bright coloring very highly, and a good blanket was traded at the fort for ten buffalo robes. The silver, horses, mules, and cattle, were taken to Missouri and sold.[35]

The new avenue of trade was welcomed by the Cheyenne. Horses and buffalo robes were fetching high prices in Missouri—William Bent was able to take as many as the Cheyenne could bring him. The Cheyenne no longer needed to travel long distances to realize the highest profit for their wares.

The Cheyenne's lifestyle was also much improved by the white man's goods. Sturdy iron kettles, guns, am-

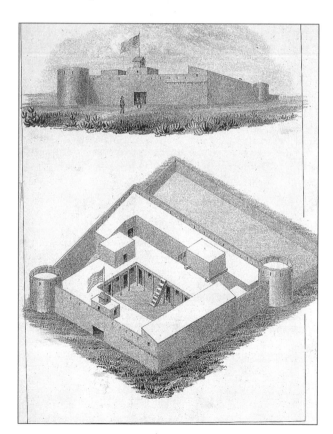

An 1845 illustration shows two views of Bent's Fort, a lucrative trading post.

A Fur Trader Speaks Openly About the Alcohol Trade

James P. Beckwourth was a unique man, one of only a few fur traders who were half African American. He had many exciting experiences over the course of his career, and in 1855 he documented his experiences in *The Life and Times of James P. Beckwourth*. Following is his justification for the use of alcohol as a trade staple:

"The sale of liquor is one of the most profitable branches of a trader's business, and, since the appetite for the vile potion had already been created, my personal influence in the matter was very slight. I was no law-giver; I was no longer in a position to prohibit the introduction of the white man's firewater; if I had refused to sell it to the Indians, plenty more traders would have furnished it to them, and my conscientious scruples would benefit the Indians none, and would deprive my embarrassed employer of a very considerable source of profit."

Alcohol was a popular trade item on the Plains.

munition in great quantities, knives, iron for their arrowheads, glass beads, colorful cloth and blankets, coffee, and sugar—the Cheyenne were living better than they ever had before.

Cheyenne parents encouraged marriages between the fur traders and their daughters, hoping the relationship would cement their future with the whites. William Bent produced four children from his two Cheyenne marriages. Fur trader John S. Smith was father to Jack, the screeching toddler who caught Garrard's attention. Not only were fur traders enriching the Cheyenne materially, but they were enriching the tribe's population. The Cheyenne were confident that the union between the two cultures—Indian and white—would strengthen their tribe.

A Good Thing Goes Bad

That union soon proved detrimental. The Cheyenne, now in close contact with the whites, were exposed to monstrous diseases

The Great Peace of 1840

Many a pitched battle was fought against the other Plains tribes. The Comanche, Kiowa, and Plains Apache were determined that the southern Cheyenne bands return to the Black Hills. War between these tribes was frequent in the first quarter of the nineteenth century, and countless warriors died in the bloody engagements. In the late 1830s, two especially violent battles convinced these tribes that they needed to live in peace.

The Great Peace of 1840 was a formal affair. Gifts were exchanged at a crossing on the Arkansas River. Pledges of friendship were made, leading "to a lasting amity among the high plains tribes— Cheyennes, Arapahoes, [Teton Sioux], Comanches, Kiowas, and Plains Apaches," writes Elliot West in *The Contested Plains*. "For twenty years Colorado east of the Rockies had been mostly a neutral ground, country that several groups wanted but none could fully control. In 1840 it became the common hunting and camping terrain of a broad alliance of former enemies."

for which they had no tolerance. Measles and whooping cough were the first to attack, killing many Cheyenne in 1845 and scarring and weakening others. In 1849, after being exposed to cholera, "men and women were stricken by the 'big cramps,'"[36] according to Berthrong, falling in agony from their horses and dying. As many as half their people died in 1849.

Alcohol was another goblin. The Cheyenne liked whiskey. It made them feel happy, brave, and strong, all at the same time. However, they liked it too much. Many became addicted to alcohol, and unscrupulous traders took advantage of this addiction. One robe, representing a week's labor, was traded for a pint of whiskey, which was generally consumed in one sitting. Worse yet, some Cheyenne became violent when they drank. The wives of these men hid with their children whenever alcohol was available.

Disease and alcohol were only the beginning. By encouraging fur traders to establish trading posts in their country, the Cheyenne invited a deluge of white men. The first few visitors were welcomed by the Cheyenne. But when the United States won its war with Mexico in the late 1840s, the Pacific coast opened for settlement and emigrants flooded into Cheyenne territory. Wagon trains snaked along trails to the Pacific.

Even so, those first emigrants were merely an annoying trickle of white faces beneath billowing white canvas, and the

Cheyenne did not mind them crossing their land. As long as the emigrants did not attempt to settle, the Cheyenne left them alone.

The Lure of Gold

In 1849 the trickle became a steady stream. Gold had been discovered in California. Emigrants who had previously been afraid to tackle the Great Plains became newly courageous when the dream turned golden. These emigrants, called the forty-niners, came to Cheyenne country by the tens of thousands. Although their intent was merely to cross, they exacted a devastating toll on the land. Historian Ralph K. Andrist explains:

> The tremendous stream of westering humanity, plodding along day after day across the rutted sod, fouled the land and drove away the buffalo and other game. The way was littered with discarded tools, clothing, furniture, broken-down wagons, food of all kinds, thrown out as equipment broke down and baggage was discarded to compensate for the reduced pulling power of weakening animals. Animals gave out and died; the fresh smell of spring grass was blotted out by the corruption of rotting flesh.[37]

The Cheyenne were pulled in two directions. They did not want to offend the white man—they liked his trade goods. However, they were angered at what was being done to their land. They were glad when few white men stayed and hoped the stream would one day run dry.

It did not. Three hundred thousand emigrants crossed the plains between 1841 and 1859. In the spring of 1859, the stream swelled to a cascading river when gold was discovered in Colorado. The following year alone, a hundred thousand

Forty-niners pan for gold during the 1849 California gold rush.

A frontier family on their westward migration. Between 1841 and 1860, four hundred thousand emigrants crossed the plains.

fifty-niners chased golden dreams across the central Great Plains, but this time was different. This time they stayed.

In 1859 the Cheyenne began to have serious difficulties. Buffalo were scarce that summer. Drought, overhunting, and diseases carried by domestic stock had severely thinned the herds. When the Cheyenne went to their favorite camps that winter, they were dismayed at what they found. The timber had been destroyed to feed the emigrants' fires. Even Big Timbers was a mere stand of trees. The grass was gone; the emigrants' oxen and horses had stripped it away, roots and all. The 1859 Cheyenne winter camps were popu-

lated with cold, hungry people and starving horses.

Over the next fifteen years, similar gold strikes were made in two other Great Plains territories: Montana and Dakota. The river of emigrants became a raging torrent. Miners flooded onto the plains, blazing new trails. Following the miners came the merchants. On the heels of the merchants came the town builders. The busy city of Denver sprang up at the western edge of Cheyenne territory. The Cheyenne, increasingly less tolerant, began raiding wagon trains. The United States military reacted by building forts and garrisoning them with troops. By the early 1860s, Cheyenne hunting parties were more likely to encounter a company of soldiers than a single buffalo.

A Nation Divided

The unity of the Cheyenne Nation suffered. Disease had killed many—an entire band was wiped out in an 1849 cholera epidemic. Alcohol had destroyed many good warriors and weakened their civilization. Homicide, suicide, domestic abuse—all the crimes forbidden by Sweet Medicine had become commonplace. Winters were to be feared, with most of the

Cheyenne and Arapaho: Yin and Yang

Where there were Cheyenne, there were bound to be Arapaho. The relationship between these two tribes had been forged way back during their mutual days on the upper Missouri River. In fact, many experts maintain that the Cheyenne followed the Arapaho onto the Great Plains.

There were several reasons for this tight alliance. Both tribes spoke a dialect of the same language, Algonquian. Both tribes were small, with populations hovering around three thousand. Allied together, they were able to occupy and control the central Great Plains, preventing the encroachment of other tribes. The Cheyenne may have been the bolder of the two, though.

Historian Ralph K. Andrist analyzes the relationship in *The Long Death: The Last Days of the Plains Indians*, explaining: "It was the Cheyennes who were the leaders in the confederation; they had a stronger tribal organization and a more highly developed culture, and the easy-going Arapahoes were usually content to follow where their Cheyenne partners pointed the way. Both were brave opponents in war, the Cheyennes especially fought with a courage and dash that often bordered on fanaticism."

A Cheyenne and Arapaho council. The two allied tribes controlled the central Great Plains.

warm robes traded for alcohol and the timbers stripped by the emigrants. The Cheyenne had to ride thin horses a long way to find buffalo.

By 1859 the stressed Cheyenne Nation was torn in two. In their avoidance of the white man, certain bands stayed in the north, allying themselves with the Northern Arapaho and the Teton Sioux. Other bands stayed well to the south, allying themselves with the Southern Arapaho, the Comanche, the Kiowa, and the Plains Apache. According to Berthrong, "One group lived between the North and South Platte Rivers, the other between the latter stream and the Arkansas. The settlers and routes to the gold fields along the South Platte placed barriers between the two divisions and began limiting the freedom of movement between the two groups."[38]

The Cheyenne were no longer unified. They were divided into Northern and Southern Cheyenne. Over the subsequent two decades, each tribe would fight its own battles and sign its own treaties, much to the confusion of the United States government.

Chapter 5

The Cheyenne Wars: 1857 to 1878

War between the Cheyenne and the United States was inevitable. They were two nations determined to possess the same territory and both bent on sole ownership. And there was never any doubt that the United States would win. Its superiority in numbers and weapons made it by far the strongest force. The Cheyenne's biggest strength, however, lay in their determination. They were prepared to die holding on to their country, which made them more formidable than government soldiers imagined. Determination, however, did not prove to be enough. The Cheyenne put up a great fight, but ultimately they lost and were confined to reservations.

The Initial Skirmishes

The conflict between the United States government and the Cheyenne, known as the Cheyenne Wars, began when the United States military was sent to punish the Teton Sioux for having killed some soldiers at Fort Laramie in Wyoming.

United States soldiers, unable to distinguish between different tribes, directed some of their hostility toward the Cheyenne, long allied with the Sioux. Andrist explains, "On several occasions, when young braves on the plains met detachments of cavalry on patrol, they approached after making the peace sign as they had been doing for years, only to be shot at by the troopers."[39] Angered by this treatment, the Cheyenne's relations with the United States became tense.

A year later, in April 1856, the tension escalated when a United States military officer attempted to arrest three Cheyenne who were in the possession of stolen horses. The three men escaped, fleeing west to South Dakota and killing an innocent fur trapper on the way. Two months later Cheyenne and Arapaho raiders attacked a wagon train, and an emigrant was killed. When the men suspected of committing this raid came to Fort Kearny, a United States military officer arrested three of them. They escaped, but one was

Treaties Made; Treaties Broken

The Cheyenne signed their first agreement with the United States in 1825. This treaty was a simple acknowledgment of U.S. sovereignty and its role in regulating trade and was only the first of many treaties the Northern and Southern Cheyenne would sign. All would be broken, either by the whites or by the war leaders who had refused to sign them. Five other important treaties are listed as follows:

1851: The Fort Laramie Treaty. The Cheyenne Nation agreed to occupy the land between the North Platte and Arkansas Rivers. Yellow Wolf was one of four Cheyenne representatives.

1861: The Treaty of Fort Wise. The Southern Cheyenne ceded the land awarded in 1851 and agreed to occupy an especially unfertile tract of land along the Purgatoire River. Black Kettle and White Antelope were two of the signers.

1865: The Treaty of the Little Arkansas. The Cheyenne agreed to occupy a reservation in Indian Territory (Oklahoma). Black Kettle was one of the signers.

1867: The Treaty of Medicine Lodge. Again the Cheyenne were assigned a reservation in Indian Territory, with hunting rights as far north as the Arkansas River. Some of the war leaders signed this treaty, as did Black Kettle.

1868: The Fort Laramie Treaty (or Red Cloud's Treaty). The Northern Cheyenne agreed to settle with the Teton Sioux on a large reservation in western South Dakota. However, those who were hostile never accepted the treaty, agency, or annuities.

In 1871 the U.S. Congress ceased making treaties with Native American nations. The president of the United States became responsible for establishing reservations and terms of surrender and agreement.

---

badly wounded. As a result, the Cheyenne were angry and determined to retaliate. In the words of George Bent:

Two unprovoked attacks had been made on the Cheyennes by the troops; and now the young men began to raid on the Platte Road. Several war parties left the camps and went up to the Platte. They captured a large wagon train east of Kearny and another farther up the river; and by the end of September they had made so many attacks on small parties of travelers that the road was no longer safe except for large trains of armed men.[40]

The United States government could not allow these raids to go unpunished, so it turned its attention from the Sioux to the Cheyenne, sending Colonel E. V. Sumner and two companies of soldiers to fight the Cheyenne. On July 29, 1857, a battle took place on the Solomon River in northwestern Kansas. The Cheyenne were beaten by Sumner's men, and those who survived fled south. Sumner continued onward, burning their abandoned village before returning to Fort Leavenworth.

Cheyenne peace chiefs met with William Bent to discuss the tribe's problems with the whites. The fur trader advised them to avoid further angering the United States military, but the peace chiefs were not certain they could do this, given the influence of the war leaders. "They would do what they could to keep matters under control, they said," according to West, "but they were having increasing difficulty controlling their younger men, who chafed at the treatment and humiliations."[41] The peace chiefs did persevere, however; and on February 18, 1861, the Southern Cheyenne peace chiefs signed a treaty with the United States government, accepting a reservation in Colorado.

The Southern Cheyenne Are Engaged

Those peace chiefs did not speak for the entire Southern Cheyenne tribe, though, and no Southern Cheyenne war leaders were present at the signing of the 1861 treaty. As a result, the chiefs had

no control over the raiding war leaders, and the treaty was ineffective. Nebraska State Historical Society archivist Dr. Donald F. Danker explains, describing the war as

Colonel Edwin Vose Sumner defeated the Cheyenne in an 1857 battle.

a series of skirmishes, punitive campaigns, scouting and patrolling expeditions, conducted by the United States Army against tribesmen who one month might be peaceably receiving annuities at their agency and the next raiding traffic and installations along the overland trails or hunting in areas to which they were prohibited entry by treaty agreement.[42]

Although the Southern Cheyenne war leaders tried to avoid direct conflicts with United States citizens, they did not feel bound to the treaty. They and their followers continued to live as they always had, hunting the same territory and camping in

An Endless Night

George Bent, son of William Bent and a Cheyenne woman, was a survivor of the Sand Creek Massacre. Although a bullet broke his hip, he was able to crawl away to safety. Years later, he told historian George E. Hyde the story of his endless night on the Plains. Hyde shared Bent's experience in *Life and Times of George Bent*.

"There we were on that bleak, frozen plain, without any shelter whatever and not a stick of wood to build a fire with. Most of us were wounded and half naked; even those who had had time to dress when the attack came, had lost their buffalo robes and blankets during the fight. The men and women who were not wounded worked all through the night, trying to keep the children and the wounded from freezing to death. They gathered grass by the handful, feeding little fires around which the wounded and the children lay; they stripped off their own blankets and clothes to keep us warm, and some of the wounded who could not be provided with other covering were buried under piles of grass which their friends gathered, a handful at a time. . . . It was bitter cold, the wind had a full sweep over the ground on which we lay, and in spite of everything that was done, no one could keep warm. All through the night the Indians kept hallooing to attract the attention of those who had escaped from the village to the open plain and were wandering about in the dark, lost and freezing. Many who had lost wives, husbands, children, or friends, went back down the creek and crept over the battleground among the naked and mutilated bodies of the dead. Few were found alive, for the soldiers had done their work thoroughly; but now and then during that endless night some man or woman would stagger in among us, carrying some wounded person on their back."

their old favorite campsites. As more and more whites settled in Cheyenne territory, this refusal to abandon their old freedom threw the Southern Cheyenne warriors into close proximity with United States citizens. Trouble was brewing, and only a catalyst was needed to ignite a major conflict between the two nations.

That catalyst occurred in the spring of 1864. In the words of West, "A year of bloodshed began on April 12, 1864, when troops exchanged fire with several Dog Soldiers accused of stealing four mules."[43] Then in May a lieutenant in the U.S. Army found a 250-lodge Cheyenne village. This peaceful village was home to Lean Bear and Black Kettle, longtime peace chiefs for the Southern Cheyenne. When Lean Bear rode forward to show the lieutenant the peace medal he had received in Washington, D.C., the soldiers shot him. The Cheyenne were outraged at the unprovoked assassination, and this incident gave the Southern Cheyenne warriors ample cause to retaliate.

The Sand Creek Massacre

After Lean Bear's assassination, the warriors went on a rampage, killing homesteaders, soldiers, wagon drivers—any white unfortunate to cross their path. When the warriors cut off the supply and mail routes into the city of Denver, Colorado's citizens became especially frightened. The governor of Colorado Territory, John Evans, took immediate action. He began assembling a force of Colorado volunteers to fight the Cheyenne. He ordered all peaceful Indians to gather at the military forts closest to them and authorized the citizens of Colorado Territory to kill any Indians deemed hostile.

Colonel John Chivington was placed in charge of the volunteer force. Chivington was, according to Angie Debo, author of *A History of the Indians of the United States*, "a ruthless Indian-hater with political ambitions."[44] On September 28, 1864, the Southern Cheyenne peace chief Black Kettle visited Chivington and asked for peace, but the colonel told him that the only way to achieve peace would be for all Cheyenne to surrender, laying down their arms. Black Kettle knew the Cheyenne could not relinquish their arms; to do so would jeopardize their lives and livelihood. However, he did agree to lead his band to Fort Lyons in compliance with Governor Evans's orders. On November 2, 1864, the United States government ordered them to move again, this time to Sand Creek, an area forty miles from Fort Lyons.

Then on the morning of November 29, 1864, Colonel Chivington and seven hundred U.S. soldiers attacked Black Kettle's camp at Sand Creek, killing 164 men, women, and children. According to anthropologist James A. Mooney, Chivington and his army committed atrocities "never exceeded by the worst savages in America."[45] Cheyenne were shot in the back as they fled. Children were lured from hiding places and clubbed to death. Black Kettle grabbed an American flag and waved it frantically at the soldiers,

U.S. soldiers, led by Colonel John Chivington, charge into Black Kettle's camp at Sand Creek. One hundred sixty-four Cheyenne were slaughtered in the brutal, unprovoked assault.

but they continued shooting. Black Kettle fled with his wife, who was shot nine times. Amazingly, both she and her husband survived.

The War Leaders Retaliate

Word of the massacre traveled fast, and soon Cheyenne war leaders all across the Great Plains heard about the unprovoked attack on a peaceful Cheyenne camp. They responded quickly. Berthrong reports:

The survivors of the Sand Creek Massacre fled to join their kinsmen on the Smoky Hill River. Practically the whole of the Southern Cheyenne tribe was in these camps, re-enforced by the Dog Soldier band. Runners were quickly sent to their allies,

Spotted Tail's and Pawnee Killer's people of the Sioux and the Northern Arapahoes. Even those Cheyennes previously friendly to the whites now thirsted for white blood and vengeance.[46]

On January 6, 1865, more than one thousand warriors raided up and down the Platte road in retaliation for the Sand Creek Massacre. They burned ranches, stole cattle, and killed as many as a hundred whites. At the beginning of February, the combined tribes headed north and fought the whites in the Powder River country of Wyoming and Montana. When fall came, the Southern Cheyenne returned to the south and peacefully hunted before heading for their winter camps.

Investigation and Treaties

While the Cheyenne were raiding in retaliation for the Sand Creek Massacre, the United States government was investigating the incident. Regarding the findings of this investigation, Andrist says, "of the 33 witnesses who testified, 14 supported Chivington, 17 condemned him. Most of those who spoke against him had been his own boys."[47] The U.S. government decided that the Cheyenne had been unfairly attacked. In an attempt to right this wrong, it sent a team of negotiators to make a treaty with the Southern Cheyenne. One article of this treaty promised restitution to those whose relatives had died at Sand Creek. The negotiators were successful, and seven leaders, including Black Kettle, signed the Treaty of the Little Arkansas on October 14, 1865.

Although many of the war leaders refused to recognize this treaty, they and their followers had begun to calm down by the spring of 1867. However, the calm was short-lived. Later that spring, the military sent Major Winfield Scott Hancock into the field. Hancock's purpose was merely to impress the Cheyenne with the power of the United States military, not to attack or otherwise upset them. However, he made the mistake of camping too near a Cheyenne village. When the Indians "abandoned their village and fled in the night, fearing another Sand Creek,"[48] according to West, Hancock thought they had left to raid settlers, and he ordered their village burned. The Cheyenne war leaders took exception, and hostilities were renewed.

Once again, the United States sent negotiators, this time in the form of a special peace commission. President Grant had assumed office, and upon the advice of several religious officials, he decided that peace, not war, was the answer to the Cheyenne problem. The commission was successful in convincing the peace chiefs and a few of the militant bands to move to a reservation in Oklahoma, then known as Indian Territory. In the fall of 1867, the Treaty of Medicine Lodge was signed. "Among the names of those Cheyennes signing the papers were Black Kettle and Little Robe, acknowledged leaders of the peace faction," writes Berthrong, "and Bull Bear, Tall Bull, White Horse, and Whirlwind, chiefs of the soldier societies."[49]

The Southern Cheyenne Rise Again

The new peace was short-lived, however. Mooney writes, "Notwithstanding the treaty and their peaceful professions, the Southern Cheyenne and Arapaho, in the summer of 1868, suddenly began a series of raids and outrages in Kansas, for which this time there was not a shadow of provocation. . . ."[50] There was no catalyst propelling the Cheyenne into violence this time, although one army lieutenant blamed easy access to whiskey for the raids. Whatever the cause, the Cheyenne renegades attacked whites living in the valleys of the Saline and Solomon Rivers.

Roman Nose

Roman Nose was one of the greatest of all Cheyenne warriors. He was believed to have incredibly powerful medicine, and legend says that because of his powers, Roman Nose could fight courageously, even recklessly, and never suffer an injury. Once he rode so near the enemy line, his pony was shot from beneath him, but he received not even a scratch.

The secret to Roman Nose's alleged power lay in his famous war bonnet, given to him by a powerful Cheyenne priest. Both Roman Nose and the priest had shared a similar dream, that with a special war bonnet, Roman Nose would be invulnerable to bullets and arrows. The priest made the warrior a war bonnet according to this dream. He also instructed Roman Nose in the ways of life necessary to ensure the war bonnet retained its power. One of his instructions was that the warrior never eat any food that had been touched by a metal utensil, such as a pot or a spoon.

In September 1868, Roman Nose made a fatal mistake. He ate stew prepared for him by a Sioux woman unfamiliar with his restrictions. She had stirred the stew with a metal spoon. When he discovered the mistake, he knew he would need to purify himself before he fought again. Just then, Roman Nose learned that a pitched battle was being waged near the camp, at a place now known as Beecher's Island. When he told the messenger that he could not fight that day, the man pleaded with him. The battle was going poorly. The Cheyenne could not win without Roman Nose's great power.

Roman Nose agreed. Knowing he rode to his death, he painted his face, donned his famous war bonnet, and mounted his pony. He did not return.

Roman Nose, a Cheyenne warrior whose war bonnet was said to render him impervious to enemy fire.

Custer's troops attack Black Kettle's camp during the Battle of Washita. Black Kettle and more than one hundred other Cheyenne died in the battle.

General Philip Sheridan commanded an expedition against the renegades in the winter of 1868–69. In November he sent Lieutenant Colonel George Armstrong Custer against Black Kettle's camp on the Washita River in western Oklahoma. West notes that the ensuing battle was fierce, writing, "A portion of Custer's attackers was isolated and wiped out, but the Cheyennes lost more than 100 persons, including Black Kettle and his wife."[51] The Cheyenne warriors responded to Black Kettle's death with renewed vigor, concentrating their attacks against settlers in Nebraska until the state requested and was given military protection by the United States government.

The battles finally ended on July 11, 1869, when the Fifth Cavalry, aided by fifty Pawnee scouts, surprised most of the Dog Soldiers at Summit Springs in western Colorado. Separated from their ponies and greatly outnumbered, the Dog Soldiers were forced to fight to the death. Many important war leaders lost their lives that day, and the back of the warrior faction was broken. The renegade Southern Cheyenne were escorted to their Oklahoma reservation.

The Northern Cheyenne Hold On

The Northern Cheyenne, however, continued to fight. Since the beginning of the nineteenth century, the Northern Cheyenne had been allied with the fierce Teton Sioux, and during the 1860s, they had fought together in Red Cloud's War, protesting the establishment of military forts in Wyoming and Montana. This war was the only time in the history of the plains that a tribe successfully fought the United States government. As a result, the Northern Cheyenne, the Sioux, and the Northern Arapaho were given a large reservation encompassing most of western South Dakota.

Then gold was discovered there. "Miners swarmed into the Indian country," according to historian Robert M. Utley, "and the government, making only a token effort to keep them out, hesitantly broached the subject of buying the part of the reservation that contained the Black Hills."[52] When its offer was refused, the U.S. government declared war on the three tribes, ordering them to stay on the reservation in South Dakota and giving them until January 1, 1876, to comply.

When the Cheyenne, Arapaho, and Sioux did not comply, the U.S. military was sent to bring them in. On June 17, 1876, the Cheyenne fought valiantly alongside the Sioux, repelling the U.S. military at the Battle of Rosebud. On June 25, 1876, they fought again in the battle

Buffalo Calf Road Woman

The battle at Rosebud Creek on June 17, 1876, was a victory for the Cheyenne and the Sioux. Most historians call this the Battle of Rosebud. The Cheyenne, however, have another name for it.

Comes in Sight was a valiant Cheyenne warrior, one who took many chances, one unafraid to engage the enemy where they were the strongest. When he fought the white soldiers at Rosebud Creek, he was, as always, right in the thick of things. His sister, Buffalo Calf Road Woman, surely must have feared for him several times while she watched the battle from her place of concealment in the trees.

Then the unthinkable happened. Comes in Sight's horse was shot. As it plummeted to the ground, it flung the warrior over its head. Landing agilely on his feet, Comes in Sight began a desperate footrace through the battle lines, dodging bullets, arrows, and enemy soldiers. No one thought he would make it. His comrades were too busy fighting U.S. soldiers to worry about saving him.

Perhaps combatants on both sides paused for a split second to focus on the horse and rider streaking to Comes in Sight's aid. Sliding her horse to a halt beside her brother, Buffalo Calf Road Woman urged him to mount. Comes in Sight leaped up behind her, and the two raced away to safety. That is why the Cheyenne call this particular engagement the Battle Where the Sister Saved Her Brother.

known as the Battle of the Little Bighorn, or Custer's Last Stand. That battle marked the end for Custer when he made two strategic errors: he did not send scouts to determine the size of the Indian camp nestled along the Little Bighorn River in Montana, and he did not wait for reinforcements before attacking.

Sending one-third of his men to scout for more Indians and a second third to attack the village from the southwest end, Custer raced with the rest of his men to the northeast end, where the Cheyenne were camped. He never got there. The camp he chose to attack stretched for three miles and was the largest Indian camp ever gathered on the western plains. Custer had not yet reached its end when he and his 225 men were attacked by hundreds of warriors. The order was given to dismount, and the soldiers fought standing. John Stands in Timber describes the battle as follows:

George Armstrong Custer was killed at the Battle of the Little Bighorn.

At the end it was quite a mess. They could not tell which was this man or that man, they were so mixed up. Horses were running over the soldiers and over each other. The fighting was really close, and they were shooting almost any way without taking aim. . . . After they emptied their pistols this way there was no time to reload. Neither side did. But most of the Indians had clubs or hatchets, while the soldiers just had guns.[53]

In less than thirty minutes, Custer and his men were dead.

The Destruction of Dull Knife's Camp

After the Battle of the Little Bighorn, the United States military was determined to punish the Cheyenne for their part in the battle. On November 25, 1876, the government got its chance.

Cheyenne peace chief Dull Knife and his band were camped in the Powder River country of Montana when U.S. soldiers stumbled upon them while searching for the Sioux. The Northern Cheyenne were not prepared for an attack. In fact, the band had been having internal problems all day. A priest named Box Elder had warned Dull Knife and all the camp leaders that they needed to move. Box Elder had seen a vision of many approaching soldiers. The Cheyenne were convinced because Box Elder's medicine was strong; he had not yet been wrong. They saddled their horses and began packing their goods on travois.

The Kit Foxes warrior society intervened, however, placing the camp under military rule. They had had good success in hunting that day and wanted to celebrate. Some Cheyenne did try to resist. However, the Kit Foxes cut the saddles off the horses of some and whipped others. So the Cheyenne remained in camp despite Box Elder's warning, and within hours the camp was destroyed. In the words of Powell:

> Most of the old Northern Cheyenne material beauty died in the flames of Morning Star's [Dull Knife's] camp. Two hundred tipis, nearly all of canvas, but some of buffalo hide, were destroyed. Among them were elaborately decorated lodges of the military societies, their linings covered with vividly colored paintings of men and horses moving in battle. Exquisitely quilled and beaded clothing, the sacred shields, scalp shirts and war-bonnets—all were carried off or burned. . . . Never again would Northern Cheyenne material culture reach the heights of richness and splendor that the people knew before that bitter day in the Big Horns.[54]

Similar campaigns were launched against the remaining Northern Cheyenne, mostly night attacks in the deep of winter, when they were at their most vulnerable. Their lodges, robes, and winter supplies burned, their ponies dying from hunger, the Northern Cheyenne finally surrendered in 1877. The Cheyenne Wars were over.

Chapter 6

Early Days on the Reservation

The United States had won the war. The Cheyenne were defeated. Once the United States had the land it coveted, the surviving Cheyenne became part of what the government called "the Indian Problem." Until the Cheyenne were assimilated, or absorbed, into American society, they were to be treated as prisoners of war, confined to a reservation patrolled by the U.S. military and supervised by the Bureau of Indian Affairs (BIA). This made the Cheyenne dependent on the U.S. government for sustenance, clothing, and shelter. The government, however, was stingy. It did not like spending money on Indians.

The Southern Cheyenne Starve

Stinginess resulted in hunger. In 1875 the Southern Cheyenne and the Southern Arapaho were confined to a reservation in Oklahoma, then known as Indian Territory.

The BIA established an agency and hired an agent to oversee all operations on the reservation, including the distribution of rations. Too often, though, the rations did not arrive, and when they were delivered, there was never enough.

Although they were hungry most of the time, the Southern Cheyenne were fortunate in one respect—they had a good agent.

Northern Cheyenne and an interpreter on a reservation near Dodge City, Kansas, in 1878.

The Origins of the Buffalo

Because the American bison were slaughtered before anyone could conduct a serious study of their habits, not much is known about their early migration patterns. It is generally believed that, similar to many birds, they migrated slowly north in the spring and slowly back south in the fall. They may have spent their summers in the cool, bug-free northern Great Plains and their winters in the warm south.

However, as late as the 1880s, the Cheyenne and the Arapaho had another explanation for the presence of the buffalo in the north and in the south. It was their belief that the buffalo originated in two caves in the Texas Panhandle. Each spring, these caves gave birth to countless buffalo. The buffalo were a gift from Maheo to the most deserving tribe, and their migration patterns steered them in the direction of Maheo's choosing. Stone Calf, a renowned reservation chief for the Southern Cheyenne, claimed to have seen these caves many, many times. He described having seen the buffalo spill forth by the thousands. When his people were starving on the Oklahoma reservation, he begged for permission to visit these caves. Permission was denied.

Buffalo, the traditional food of the Cheyenne, graze on a modern wildlife refuge in Oklahoma.

Agent John D. Miles was frustrated when rations were late or inadequate. However, he could only do so much. Miles's letters to his superiors were ignored. He demanded cattle from huge herds illegally grazing on reservation land, but when the cattlemen complained, Miles had to back down because he lacked the authority to make the demands. He borrowed food from the military at Fort Reno until supplies ran low. He issued permits for traders to supply ammunition, but the permits were revoked when local citizens complained; they were wary of arming a previously militant tribe. In 1877 Miles finally received permission for the Cheyenne to leave the reservation to hunt, but there were not enough buffalo left to feed them.

Colonel Richard I. Dodge was stationed in the area at this time. In the following excerpt from a book published in 1883, he describes the plight of the reservation Indians:

> Every military post in the Indian country is besieged by these starving people. The slop-barrels and dump-piles are carefully scrutinized, and stuff that a cur [dog] would disdain is carried off in triumph. The offal [scraps] about the butcher shop is quarrelled over, and devoured raw and on the spot. The warm blood of slaughtered beeves [cattle] is sucked up by numerous mouths before it has time to sink into the ground. Every horse that dies of disease or by accident, is at once converted into meat. . . . [55]

The Southern Cheyenne were dying, some from starvation, others from diseases like influenza, malaria, tuberculosis, trachoma, measles, and smallpox that prey on those in a weakened physical condition.

In April 1877 something happened to make their situation even more dire. "Agent Miles then was informed," writes Berthrong in *The Cheyenne and Arapaho Ordeal*, "that his agency should be prepared to receive fourteen hundred Northern Cheyennes."[56]

The Northern Cheyenne Come to Oklahoma

The Northern Cheyenne did not want to go south. They had been promised reser-

Cheyenne and Sioux warriors on the Plains. The Northern Cheyenne eventually grew closer to the Sioux than to the Southern Cheyenne.

vations with the Sioux in South Dakota, and they were friendlier with the Sioux than with the Southern Cheyenne. As early as 1865, George Bent noticed differences between the two Cheyenne tribes, writing, "They [the Northern Cheyenne] were growing more like the Sioux in habits and appearance every year. They did not dress like us at all, and their language was changing. They used many words that were strange to us."[57] Only promises of plentiful food and annuities could compel these people to journey south, which is what the U.S. government promised.

The instant they set foot in Oklahoma Territory, the Northern Cheyenne realized their error. When they saw their southern kindred starving, they knew the whites had lied about the food. When they saw threadbare canvas tepees and sickly toddlers, the Northern Cheyenne were frightened. It was not long before they, too, were hungry, and it was not long before they, accustomed to brisk nights and harsh winters, succumbed in large numbers to warm-weather diseases like malaria. The Northern Cheyenne were sick in body and heart. They asked to go home.

The U.S. government refused, wanting all Cheyenne on the same reservation. It did not matter that the Northern Cheyenne longed for the sight of black hills rising into blue northern skies. The Northern Cheyenne

were now properly in Indian Territory, and there they would stay. When they threatened to escape, the government was not worried. Home lay almost a thousand miles to the north, through country settled by farmers and ranchers and patrolled by soldiers.

The Saga of Dull Knife and Little Wolf

In September 1878, three hundred Northern Cheyenne made good on their threat to escape. At their head rode Dull Knife and Lit-

Dull Knife, one leader of the Northern Cheyenne escape from Oklahoma.

tle Wolf, the two wisest of all Northern Cheyenne peace chiefs. Mile after torturous mile, these chiefs led their people home. There were skirmishes with soldiers and ranchers along the way, skirmishes the travelers won despite limited ammunition. The United States sent troops after them, but the Cheyenne persevered. When several whites were killed in Kansas by Cheyenne during their passage, the manhunt intensified. Still the Northern Cheyenne made it to Nebraska by mid-October. There the two chiefs differed. Dull Knife wanted to join the Sioux in South Dakota; Little Wolf wanted to go to Yellowstone country. The brave travelers wished each other well and parted amicably.

Dull Knife's journey ended soon after the split. In a blinding November blizzard, he and his 168 followers walked into a company of soldiers. They were taken to Camp Robinson in Nebraska. On January 4, 1879, the commanding officer told them they would be returned to the much-loathed Oklahoma. The captives refused, saying they would rather die. In an attempt to encourage them to change their minds, the military cut off their food and water. For five frigid January days, Dull Knife's band shivered in open barracks, scraping frost from the windows to try to quench their thirst, burning floorboards for heat, and starving. They continued to maintain that they would rather die than go south. Secretly, however, they were

Little Wolf successfully led his band to Montana.

planning an escape.

On the evening of January 9, 1879, the Northern Cheyenne broke out of their military prison and fled into the night. During the next two weeks, sixty-four Cheyenne were killed and seventy-eight were recaptured. Twenty-seven managed to escape, including Dull Knife, and they ultimately joined their Sioux friends on the Pine Ridge Reservation in southwestern South Dakota.

Little Wolf's band fared better than Dull Knife's. Because they wintered along the Niobrara River, it was not until March

Genocide

When looking back in time, it can be difficult to comprehend attitudes. Without the proper perspective, there is a tendency to disbelieve the truly amazing. For example, it seems ludicrous today that citizens of a democratic nation could actually propose genocide, the extermination of an entire race. However, many United States citizens believed this practice was the only logical solution to the so-called Indian Problem. A closer look at contemporary attitudes can be found in the literature of the day. Fur trader James P. Beckwourth offers an excellent perspective in his 1855 book *The Life of James P. Beckwourth*, in which he candidly discusses the logistics of genocide.

"If it is the policy of government to utterly exterminate the Indian race, the most expeditious manner of effecting this ought to be the one adopted. The introduction of whisky among the Red Men, under the connivance of government agents, leads to the demoralization and consequent extermination, by more powerful races, of thousands of Indians annually. Still, this infernal agent is not effectual; the Indians diminish in numbers, but with comparative slowness. The most direct and speedy mode of clearing the land of them would be by the simple means of starvation—by depriving them of their hereditary sustenance, the buffalo. To effect this, send an army of hunters among them, to root out and destroy, in every possible manner, the animal in question. They can shoot them, poison them, dig pit-falls for them, and resort to numberless other contrivances to efface the devoted animal, which serves, it would seem, by the wealth of its carcass, to preserve the Indian, and thus impede the expanding development of civilization."

1879 that they encountered U.S. troops. Little Wolf surrendered, and he and his followers were taken to Fort Keogh along the Yellowstone River in Montana. Mari Sandoz, author of *Cheyenne Autumn*, stirringly depicts their arrival in the following extract:

The people stopped along the gray bluffs and looked down upon the tree-lined stream that was the Yellowstone. For a long time there was only silence, as from strangers come to a strange land. But then a trilling went up from among them somewhere, a young voice, a young girl come into a new time. Her thin, clear peal was followed by a loud resounding cry, a cry of the grown, the old, the weary, and the forlorn. . . .[58]

The Northern Cheyenne had finally come home, and this time they were allowed to remain. Some of the survivors of

Dull Knife's band remained with the Sioux in South Dakota, but in 1884 most of the Northern Cheyenne moved to a reservation in Montana.

Assimilation Begins in Earnest

Once all the Cheyenne were settled on reservations, the U.S. government intensified its efforts at assimilation. The flight of the Northern Cheyenne had convinced the government that to prevent further escapes or uprisings, the Cheyenne culture must be eradicated, once and for all. In their anthol-

Two Cheyenne men wear European-style clothing.

ogy *Native American Voices: A Reader*, editors Susan Lobo and Steve Talbot refer to this enforced assimilation as cultural genocide, explaining, "The concept of cultural genocide or *ethnocide* . . . refers to measures taken by the oppressor group to stamp out indigenous culture and its social institutions."[59]

The Cheyenne were proving to be the most troublesome of all the Plains Indians. Every time the U.S. government was certain the tribe had been defeated and accepted its new status, the Cheyenne proved them wrong by escaping or rising again. The only way to make certain the tribe did not rise again was to make certain its members forgot the old ways, forgot what it was to be Cheyenne. The best way to accomplish this was to change their appearance, eradicate their language and traditions, make them self-supporting, and get rid of their religion.

Steps Toward Assimilation

The first step was to change the Cheyenne's appearance. As most psychologists will attest, appearance is crucial to self-perception, and if the Cheyenne saw themselves in white attire, with white haircuts, the government believed they would begin to think like whites.

The next step was to take away their language and traditions. The U.S. government could not force adult Cheyenne to suddenly speak English, nor could it erase their memories. However, children could be taught to think, speak, and act like whites if taken away from their parents. The government virtually ripped these young Cheyenne from their parents' arms, sending them to boarding schools across the nation. These boarding schools had been developed specifically to meet the needs of Indian children, with an emphasis on teaching English, trade skills, and housekeeping. Moore writes, "In both Montana and Oklahoma, enrollment in boarding schools was often involuntary, and sometimes rations were withheld or threats were made by the military to force Cheyenne families to send their children away to school."[60]

It was equally important to the U.S. government that the Cheyenne become self-supporting. The sooner the men could support their families, the sooner the government would not have to pay for their care. Farming and ranching were the skills the government chose to teach them. According to Moore, "The government hired 'farmers-in-charge' in Oklahoma and Montana to teach them [the Cheyenne] how to plow, and encourage them to grow, of all things, potatoes, which were quite inappropriate for the climate and soils of both reservations."[61] Cattle were supplied for ranching, but this experiment took a long time to realize fruition. Too often, hunger forced the Cheyenne to eat their breeding stock.

Another effective means of facilitating assimilation is to strip a people of its religion and enforce upon them the religion of their conquerors. Quakers, Mennonites, and Catholics traveled to the reservations to preach the word of their deity to the

Residents of Indian Territory pose for a Sunday school portrait. Many religious groups sent missionaries to the reservations to convert the Cheyenne to Christianity.

Frederic Remington on the Southern Cheyenne

In 1891 Western artist and author Frederic Remington visited the Southern Cheyenne on their Oklahoma reservation. In an article written for *Century Magazine*, he discussed the problem of promoting self-sufficiency among them.

"Corn cannot be raised on this reservation with sufficient regularity to warrant the attempt. The rainfall is not enough, and where white men despair, I, for one, do not expect the wild Indians to continue. They have tried it and have failed, and are now very properly discouraged. Stock-raising is the natural industry of the country, and that is the proper pursuit of these people. They are only now recovering by natural increase from the reverses which they suffered in their last outbreak. It is hard for them to start cattle herds, as their ration is insufficient, and one scarcely can expect a hungry man to herd cattle when he needs the beef to appease his hunger. Nevertheless, some men have respectable herds and can afford to kill an animal occasionally without taking the stock cattle. In this particular they display wonderful forebearance, and were they properly rationed for a time and given stock cattle, there is not a doubt but in time they would become self-supporting."

Cheyenne. The missionaries spoke of their cultural heroes, of Joseph with his coat of many colors and of Adam in his garden, hoping to make the Cheyenne forget Sweet Medicine and Erect Horns. In 1883 the U.S. government outlawed most facets of the Cheyenne religion. There would be no more Medicine Lodge ceremonies, no more renewals of Mahuts, no more channeling of Maheo's energy. Soon the government hoped the Cheyenne would be as Christian as the missionaries sent to convert them.

The Dawes General Allotment Act

The final stage of assimilation was the Dawes General Allotment Act. This legislation ordered all Native Americans to break up their reservations into 160-acre parcels, with one parcel to be allotted to each family head. Whatever land was left over after all family heads had chosen their parcel would be offered for sale to United States citizens. The various tribes were asked to agree to accept allotment, but agreement was not required by law. If they disagreed, the United States would simply take their land, a contingency written into the Dawes Act.

The goal of the Dawes Act was to break up the communal lifestyle—the extended families and the villages and bands—of the Native Americans and thereby destroy their sense of community. Debo explains: "Break up their natural groupings, whether

By changing their dress and outlawing their religion and traditions, the U.S. government tried to force the Cheyenne to conform to white society.

by abolishing the governments of advanced tribes or undermining the influence of primitive chiefs, and set each family alone on a farm to develop habits of industry and the pride of possession."[62] In 1887 the United States Congress passed the Dawes Act even though the Cheyenne did not want allotment.

According to the Treaty of Medicine Lodge, however, the Southern Cheyenne did not have to comply unless three-fourths of their adult males voted in favor. So Congress

sent a commission to obtain the necessary votes. The commission, called the Jerome Commission after its chairman, was blatantly dishonest, according to both Moore and Berthrong, who maintain that the Cheyenne were swindled out of their land. By 1892 the Jerome Commission had obtained the votes necessary to force allotment on the Southern Cheyenne, who lost seven-eighths of their three-million-acre reservation.

No longer did the Southern Cheyenne own one reservation; they owned a checkerboard of allotted squares and settlement squares. "At high noon on April 19, 1892, between twenty-five and thirty-thousand settlers made a run into the Cheyenne-Arapaho Reservation," writes Berthrong, "and immediately began a new era for the Cheyennes and Arapahoes."[63] The Southern Cheyenne were not only now rubbing elbows with the whites, but more importantly, their sense of community was completely destroyed.

The Northern Cheyenne were able to resist allotment until 1931, when a special act of Congress forced them to comply. They were, in fact, the last of the Native American tribes to suffer from the Dawes Act. At that time, though, they too lost much of their land.

More and more whites were squeezing in on the Cheyenne, forcing them to behave like whites, erasing their memories of better times, starving them into submission. Their appearance, their language, their traditions, their livelihood, and their land had all been taken away. It looked like the Cheyenne

Chapter 7

An Elastic Will

In their attempts at assimilating the Cheyenne, the whites failed to take into account the Cheyenne's incredibly resilient spirit. During the Cheyenne Wars, the U.S. military stretched that spirit to breaking many times. Each time, though, the Cheyenne snapped back.

By the beginning of the twentieth century, the U.S. government was confident that it had made terrific strides in eradicating the Cheyenne's culture. The plan was that soon the Indians would be completely absorbed into white society. Soon the only way to distinguish a Cheyenne from the rest of society would be by the color of his or her skin. The Cheyenne culture would be a thing of the past. The government never got its wish.

The Cheyenne Resist Assimilation

The Cheyenne did not rise again, at least not overtly. Instead the battles they fought were silent ones. Their tactic was simple in

The Cheyenne adopted white people's clothing but retained many of their own traditions.

design: they just ignored the demand to assimilate. Admittedly, they had the appearance of white men. With their buffalo and other game gone, they could hardly refuse the clothes offered to them by the whites. However, the Cheyenne knew that appearance was only skin deep. The Cheyenne held on to the three cultural aspects that best defined them as a people: their language and traditions, the hunt, and their religion.

Unbeknownst to the U.S. government, the Cheyenne kept a tight hold on their language and traditions. Yes, their children were taken from them and sent to boarding schools. When they came home, however, their parents restored the lost language and rekindled the traditions. After visiting the

Cheyenne in 1891, Frederic Remington commented on the futility of the BIA schooling plan, saying, "They go back to the camps, go back to the blanket, let their hair grow, and forget their English. In a year one cannot tell a schoolboy from any other [Cheyenne]. . . ."[64]

Attempts to teach the Cheyenne to farm and ranch were successful, but only because the Indians genuinely wanted to support themselves. They were determined, however, to hold on to one cherished aspect of the nomadic lifestyle: the hunt. At periodic intervals, the Southern Cheyenne were issued a small lot of live steers for consumption. After each family head selected his steer, he marked it in

An 1889 drawing shows Cheyenne men hunting steer, one of the ways members kept the Cheyenne culture alive.

some manner. When all the steers had been issued and marked, the small herd was let loose onto the Oklahoma plains. The men chased them down on horseback, shooting them with arrows or bullets. Their wives followed and, as in the old days of the buffalo, processed the meat where it lay.

Religion was another aspect of the Cheyenne culture that did not die. When the Cheyenne bowed their heads to worship, it was Maheo who listened. The sacred arrows were still in the possession of the Southern Cheyenne; the buffalo hat still with the Northern Cheyenne. Ignoring the laws forbidding practice of their religion, the Northern Cheyenne began "slipping off to the privacy of the hills," according to Powell, who adds, "Maheo still heard their prayers, and the men still quietly offered their flesh as sacrifices. . . . Government eyes were not so far-seeing as to observe the Cheyennes slipping, one or two at a time, into the Sacred Hat tipi."[65] The Southern Cheyenne also held on to their ceremonies, but they did so under the guise of fairs and holiday celebrations, with BIA officials none the wiser. Maheo, Sweet Medicine, and Erect Horns were alive and well in the hearts of the Cheyenne.

By the beginning of the twentieth century, the Cheyenne had been waging their quiet battle for years. The U.S. government continued to force assimilation, and the Cheyenne continued to ignore it. Whenever the government forbade an aspect of Cheyenne heritage, the Cheyenne appeared to submit meekly while secretly continuing to do as they pleased. Each time the government stretched the elastic will of the Cheyenne, it sprang back. Then, just when the Cheyenne began to wonder how much longer they could endure, their situation began to improve.

A Fresh Beginning: The Indian Reorganization Act

World War I was over. It was a time of great national pride. The returning soldiers were lauded as national heroes, and it occurred to some patriots that not all the veterans were white. Some of the best warriors, in fact, had bronze skin. Many of these Native Americans who had fought so valiantly were not even U.S. citizens. Congress hurried to rectify the oversight, and in 1924 all Native Americans were granted citizenship status. A specially appointed commission investigated the living conditions of these new citizens and was horrified. The commission members found extreme poverty and dangerously unsanitary living conditions.

The U.S. government responded to these findings with the Indian Reorganization Act (IRA) in 1934, a genuine attempt to right some serious wrongs. There was much that was positive about the IRA. Moore writes that the IRA

called a halt to the sale of Indian Trust land and, more than that, provided money to buy back land for landless Indians. In addition, the acts contained guarantees of religious freedom for Indians, allowed them to set up their own reservation governments, and

War and War Mothers

Since early reservation times, young Cheyenne men have looked to the U.S. Armed Forces as a means of employment. Their tradition as warriors and the lack of decent employment opportunities on the reservation has made a military career doubly attractive. One result of Cheyenne involvement in active service was the emergence of the group the Cheyenne War Mothers, described by John H. Moore in *The Cheyenne:*

"Traditionally, the mothers of slain Cheyenne warriors had certain privileges and duties. They were entitled to war booty and received gifts from men in the same military society as their sons. To these ideas, after World War I, was added the Anglo-American idea of 'Gold Star Mother,' who had lost a son in the war. What emerged from this, during World War II, was the institution known as the Cheyenne War Mothers.

Organized on a community basis, war mothers in World War II included all women with sons in the military. They took responsibility for honoring their sons as they left for war and when they returned. They sponsored pow-wows to raise money for travel and gifts for soldiers, and they made special shawls for themselves with the name of their community war mothers' group and often the name, rank, and military decorations of their sons.

At the special events they sponsored, the war mothers danced as a group counter-clockwise, the opposite way from other dancers. At victory or coming-home dances, they danced clockwise with their sons. The war mothers' groups had diminished in membership after World War II, but were reorganized during the Korean and Vietnam Wars, but not during the Persian Gulf War. 'It happened too quick,' one war mother told me."

made credit available from a federal revolving fund for tribal investments.[66]

Less positive, however, was the contingency demanding that the Indians establish new, non-aboriginal governments based on constitutional law, with elected representatives.

The Cheyenne quickly took advantage of the provision concerning the repurchase of

reservation land. For the Southern Cheyenne, the buyback proved to be an uphill battle. Politics unfavorable to their quest and owners unwilling to relinquish their land seemed like insurmountable obstacles. Nevertheless, in the years after the IRA went into effect, they were able to purchase several hundred acres.

The Northern Cheyenne have been much more successful. Purchasing their old reservation lands in small increments, they managed to restore most of their reservation by 1990. It was not easy, though, according to Debo, who writes:

[In 1957] the Bureau advertised 1,340 acres of grazing land, a key area known as the Bixby Tracts, where the streams head and the main water resource of the reservation is concentrated. Three months before the sale, the tribe liquidated a cattle project for $40,000 to buy it. The Bureau, claiming the right of supervision, got control of the money and held it. As the date of the sale approached, the tribe frantically petitioned for its postponement, and members of Congress from Montana added their protest. The land was sold to a white bidder for $22,485; a year later he offered it to the Indians for $47,736, but by that time they had to use their money to bid on other allotments as they were offered.[67]

A New Government

The IRA stipulation that the tribes establish new governments was a bittersweet pill. On the one hand, the Cheyenne were happy to be allowed to govern themselves. On the other hand, the provision's emphasis on constitutional law and elected representatives stripped the old peace chiefs and war leaders of their traditional influence. Up to this point, the Cheyenne had held on to their peace chiefs and war leaders. The possibility of a new government created a chasm within the tribes, a friction between traditionalists and progressives. The traditionalists wanted to continue the old ways of turning to the peace chiefs and war leaders for advice, aid, and solace; the progressives wanted to explore

A 1924 act of Congress granting all Native Americans citizenship status was the first of many attempts to restore some of what the tribes had lost.

The power traditionally held by Cheyenne warriors (pictured) slowly faded.

larger tribe, the Southern Cheyenne were unhappy with this arrangement. But there was nothing they could do. To gain the other IRA benefits, they had to accept this stipulation.

The Northern Cheyenne, alone on their reservation, were more fortunate. They eased into the transition, forming a Tribal Council similar to the old Council of Forty-four. There was still some friction between traditionalists and progressives. The traditionalists refused to accept the loss of the peace chiefs' authority, continuing to address their concerns directly to these men, rather than at the meetings of the Tribal Council. This angered the progressives, who resented the peace chiefs' interference and their influence in swaying council votes. The passage of time has alleviated much of this friction, however, as the Northern Cheyenne adapted to the new government, becoming increasingly progressive overall. According to Northern Cheyenne John Stands in Timber,

the new ways of determining tribal policy by turning to written law and the ballot box.

In Oklahoma there was conflict between the Southern Cheyenne and the Southern Arapaho, who shared a reservation. Because the U.S. government recognized the two tribes as one confederated tribe, they were forced to form a new government together. After much arguing, the Cheyenne and Arapaho settled on a representative government. Each tribe contributed fourteen representatives to a governing community. As the

This Council has considerable authority in running Cheyenne affairs today, while the chiefs and military society members do not have any unless they happen to be Council members as well. Their influence is still important in the [Medicine Lodge] and other ceremonies, but as a whole it is slowly dying away.[68]

Indian Claims Commission

The 1944 Indian Claims Commission (ICC) was another agency that the U.S. government established to better the situation of Native Americans. Its purpose was to settle claims against the government for "fraud, treaty violations, or other wrongs done to the Indians by the government,"[69] explains Debo. Both the Northern and Southern Cheyenne were delighted. They had been wronged as much as any other tribe, and they looked forward to seeing these wrongs righted. There was, however, a catch.

In the case of land lost because of broken treaties, the value of the land was calculated at the time of the treaty, a tiny amount compared to modern values. Additionally, once the land's value had been calculated, offsets, or past tribal expenses, were applied against it. These offsets consisted of the expenses the U.S. government had incurred while caring for the Cheyenne during their entire time on the reservation, including food, clothing, and shelter. As with the IRA, the Northern and Southern Cheyenne saw very different results.

The Northern Cheyenne initiated a claim in 1948. Because they had only been on their reservation since 1884, their offsets were not huge. They were given $4 million to satisfy all their claims against the U.S. government.

The Southern Cheyenne were not so fortunate, and they are still trying to settle their many claims against the government. One of their lost-lands claims was finally settled in 1968. The value of the land at the time of the broken treaty was assessed at $20 million. However, when offsets were applied against this sum, it was determined the Southern Cheyenne actually owed the U.S. government. Rather than countersue the Southern Cheyenne for payment of this claim, the government decided to pay a small amount to each member. The ICC gave each tribal member $2,000, and the claim was closed. Other claims are still pending.

Battles Waged: Employment and Income

Throughout the twentieth century, lack of employment and low income have been long-standing problems for the Cheyenne on both reservations. Because there are few employment opportunities on the reservation, Cheyenne men and women must look elsewhere to find employment. In doing so, they leave behind their families and reservation benefits, such as health care and inexpensive housing. Low income is another problem. If the Cheyenne are fortunate enough to find a job on the reservation, the pay is usually not enough to support their families. In 1996 Moore maintained that "for nearly all their wage work, the Cheyenne have been paid less than the minimum wages established by federal law in the last 40 years. When working on farms and ranches, Cheyenne men are paid by the day. At present, they received about $20 or $30 a day, which is about half the minimum wage."[70] The average income for tribal members runs from $2,000 to $3,000 per year, well below the national poverty level. It is virtually impossible to survive on this amount, and hunger and discomfort are common.

As a result, tribespeople supplement their small incomes in several ways. The Southern Cheyenne often lease their land to cattle ranchers. They hold bingo games and sell tax-free tobacco products to nonreservation residents in the surrounding areas. Both Northern and Southern Cheyenne women earn extra money by selling Native American crafts to tourists.

The Cheyenne Today

There are many more battles to be fought. In addition to fighting poverty, the Cheyenne also must fight racism, health care problems, and a poor public education system.

The old stereotype of Indians as being less than human still exists, and Cheyenne children learn at an early age that they are in many ways different from the white people living near them. This racism influences the self-perceptions of many,

The Rebirth of the American Bison

It is estimated that in 1850 as many as twenty million buffalo roamed the Great Plains of North America. Overhunting, diseases, and unfavorable weather conditions reduced their numbers to a mere 551 by 1889. Valiant efforts were made, most notably by zoologist William Temple Hornady, to save this magnificent beast from extinction. Game preserves were established, and hunting laws were enacted. By 1960 ten thousand buffalo were alive and well in the United States, and another fifteen thousand grazed freely in Canada.

The 1970s saw a surge of interest in the buffalo when health-conscious Americans recognized the merit of its meat. A study concerning the long life spans of many of the nineteenth-century Native Americans credited their advanced age to their buffalo-meat diets, buffalo being considerably less fatty than its cousin, the cow. As a result, restaurants like The Fort in Colorado began including buffalo on their menus. Breeders began mating buffalo bulls with stock cows, creating the popular beefalo, known for the leanness of its flesh. Other private breeders began breeding the buffalo in earnest.

Today there are three hundred thousand buffalo in the United States. In 1998 an overpopulation of buffalo in Yellowstone National Park compelled park officials to issue buffalo hunting licenses for the first time. At the 2000 Denver Stock Show, a bison bull sold for a record $90,000, and a recent visit to a local Safeway in Cheyenne, Wyoming, revealed packets of buffalo burger nestling beside packets of hamburger. The Cheyenne's buffalo are obviously back, this time to stay.

Members of the Cheyenne and Arapaho tribes perform a victory war dance like the one staged by their ancestors after successful battles.

leaving emotional scars that they carry into adulthood.

Health care poses serious problems, too. Many Cheyenne, both Northern and Southern, prefer a long drive and expensive private care to dealing with the red tape and inconvenience of reservation clinics. Additionally, many Cheyenne suffer from alcoholism and diabetes, making decent health care programs all the more important.

For Cheyenne parents, securing a good education for their children is often difficult. The Southern Cheyenne in particular combat a frustrating education system. An attempt to open a reservation school failed due to lack of funds, and parents are forced to send their children to schools emphasizing European-based traditions. Although the Northern Cheyenne are more fortunate, having a reservation school for their grade school children, they, too, must send their

older children to off-reservation high schools.

Despite these problems, the Cheyenne, both Northern and Southern, continue to persevere. Against all odds, their spirit has remained wonderfully elastic, and their twentieth century ended on a positive symbolic note. In May 1999, the site of the Sand Creek Massacre, lost since 1864, was discovered by archaeologists. The following November, Native Americans of all nations gathered in Denver to memorialize those who lost their lives in the massacre. In an article in the *Denver Rocky Mountain News*, Jonny BearCub Stiffarm is quoted as saying, "I think this is a wonderful way to end the past century that has held so many tragic events for our Indian nations."[71] That citizens of Colorado, once known for their injustice to the Cheyenne, would join in commemorating the tribe's blackest day is a sign that a new century is indeed dawning.

Appendix

1680

First reported contact with whites. The Cheyenne are located on the eastern border of Wisconsin.

1806

William Rogers Clark offers a peace medal to a Cheyenne chief in western South Dakota.

1825

The Cheyenne sign their first nonaggression agreement with the United States.

1828

Yellow Wolf meets William Bent in southern Colorado.

1834

Bent's Fort, a trading post, is constructed along the Arkansas River.

1840

The Great Peace. Cheyenne, Comanche, Kiowa, and Plains Apache agree to a cessation of hostilities.

1845

The first of several epidemics strike the Cheyenne. By 1849 their numbers were reduced by half.

1849

The first of the forty-niners cross Cheyenne territory on their way west to seek gold in California.

1851

The Treaty of Fort Laramie gives the Cheyenne the region between the Platte and Arkansas Rivers.

1859

A hundred thousand fifty-niners cross Cheyenne territory on their way to the gold strikes near present-day Denver, Colorado; The Cheyenne split into two distinct divisions: Northern and Southern.

1863

Peace chief Lean Bear visits Washington, D.C.

1864

Lean Bear is killed in cold blood. The Cheyenne go on the warpath. Over 150 Cheyenne men, women, and children are massacred at Sand Creek by the U.S. military.

1867

The Treaty of Medicine Lodge confines the Southern Cheyenne to a reservation in Oklahoma.

1868

The Northern Cheyenne, along with the Teton Sioux, are triumphant against the whites. Black Kettle of the Southern Cheyenne dies at Washita.

1874

The Southern Cheyenne are again confined to a reservation.

1876

The Northern Cheyenne are victorious at Rosebud Creek and Little Bighorn River.

1877

The Northern Cheyenne surrender. Fourteen hundred make a seventy-day walk to Oklahoma.

1878

Dull Knife and Little Wolf escape, leading three hundred Cheyenne north.

1879

Dull Knife's band escapes from Camp Robinson. Sixty-four Cheyenne are killed. Little Wolf's band makes it to Montana.

1884

President Arthur signs the document giving the Northern Cheyenne their own reservation in Montana.

1887

The Dawes General Allotment Act is passed.

1891

Under coercion from the Jerome Commission, the Southern Cheyenne agree to allotments. Their reservation is opened to white settlers.

1931

The Northern Cheyenne are forced to accept allotment.

Notes

Introduction: Tsistsista, the People

1. John H. Moore, *The Cheyenne*. Cambridge, MA: Blackwell Publishers, 1996, p. 1.
2. Donald J. Berthrong, *The Southern Cheyennes*. Norman: University of Oklahoma Press, 1972, p. 4.
3. Quoted in George E. Hyde, *Life and Times of George Bent*, edited and annotated by Savoie Lottinville. Norman: University of Oklahoma Press, 1968, p. 21.

Chapter 1: The Nomadic Life

4. Elliot West, *The Contested Plains: Indians, Goldseekers, and the Rush to Colorado*. Lawrence: The University Press of Kansas, 1998, p. 40.
5. E. Adamson Hoebel, *The Cheyennes: Indians of the Great Plains*. New York: Holt, Rinehart and Winston, 1960, p. 58.
6. Berthrong, *The Southern Cheyennes*, p. 30.
7. Moore, *The Cheyenne*, p. 34.
8. Frank Gilbert Roe, *The Indian and His Horse*. Norman: University of Oklahoma Press, 1955, p. 357.
9. George Bird Grinnell, *The Cheyenne Indians, Their History and Ways of Life*, vol. 1. Lincoln: University of Nebraska Press, 1972, p. 256.

10. Grinnell, *The Cheyenne Indians*, vol. 1, p. 250.
11. West, *The Contested Plains*, p. 73.
12. Lewis H. Garrard, *Wah-to-yah and the Taos Trail*. Norman: University of Oklahoma Press, 1955, p. 114.

Chapter 2: Social and Religious Customs

13. Stan Hoig, *The Peace Chiefs of the Cheyennes*. Norman: University of Oklahoma Press, 1980, p. 14.
14. Frederic Remington, *On the Apache Indian Reservation and Artist Wanderings Among the Cheyennes*. Palmer Lake, CO: The Filter Press, 1974, p. 22.
15. Grinnell, *The Cheyenne Indians*, vol. 1, p. 66.
16. Richard I. Dodge, *Our Wild Indians*. Hartford: A. D. Worthington and Company, 1883, p. 205.
17. Hoebel, *The Cheyennes*, p. 20.
18. Garrard, *Wah-to-yah and the Taos Trail*, p. 59.
19. Dodge, *Our Wild Indians*, p. 157.
20. Peter J. Powell, *Sweet Medicine*, vol. 2. Norman: University of Oklahoma Press, 1969, p. 435.
21. Berthrong, *The Southern Cheyennes*, p. 59.

Chapter 3: War and Peace: Peace Chiefs and War Leaders

22. John Stands in Timber and Margot Liberty, *Cheyenne Memories*. Binghamton, NY: Vail-Ballou Press, 1967, p. 36.

23. West, *The Contested Plains*, p. 85.

24. Hoebel, *The Cheyennes*, p. 38.

25. Hoig, *The Peace Chiefs of the Cheyennes*, p. 8.

26. Moore, *The Cheyenne*, pp. 129–30.

27. Berthrong, *The Southern Cheyennes*, p. 68.

28. Quoted in Hyde, *Life and Times of George Bent*, pp. 338–39.

29. Dodge, *Our Wild Indians*, p. 465.

30. Powell, *Sweet Medicine*, vol. 2, p. 862.

31. Grinnell, *The Cheyenne Indians*, vol. 1, pp. 187–88.

Chapter 4: Trade and Traders

32. Moore, *The Cheyenne*, p. 71.

33. Reuben Gold Thwaites, ed., *Original Journals of the Lewis and Clark Expedition, 1804–1806*, vol. 1. New York: Arno, 1969, p. 176.

34. Powell, *Sweet Medicine*, vol. 2, p. 466.

35. Quoted in Hyde, *Life and Times of George Bent*, p. 69.

36. Berthrong, *The Southern Cheyennes*, p. 113.

37. Ralph K. Andrist, *The Long Death: The Last Days of the Plains Indians*. New York: Macmillan, 1964, p. 17.

38. Berthrong, *The Southern Cheyennes*, p. 142.

Chapter 5: The Cheyenne Wars: 1857 to 1878

39. Andrist, *The Long Death*, p. 25.

40. Quoted in Hyde, *Life and Times of George Bent*, p. 102.

41. West, *The Contested Plains*, p. 4.

42. Preface to Luther North, *Man of the Plains*, edited by Donald F. Danker. Lincoln: University of Nebraska Press, 1961, p. xii.

43. West, *The Contested Plains*, p. 287.

44. Angie Debo, *A History of the Indians of the United States*. Norman: University of Oklahoma Press, 1970, p. 191.

45. James A. Mooney, *Memoirs of the American Anthropological Association*, vol. 1. New York: Kraus Reprint Corporation, 1964, pp. 386–87.

46. Berthrong, *The Southern Cheyennes*, p. 224.

47. Andrist, *The Long Death*, p. 93.

48. West, *The Contested Plains*, p. 309.

49. Berthrong, *The Southern Cheyennes*, p. 298.

50. Mooney, *Memoirs of the American Anthropological Society*, vol. 1, p. 389.

51. West, *The Contested Plains*, p. 312.

52. Robert M. Utley, *The Indian Frontier of the American West: 1846–1890*. Albuquerque: University of New Mexico Press, 1984, p. 180.

53. Stands in Timber and Liberty, *Cheyenne Memories*, pp. 201–02.

54. Powell, *Sweet Medicine*, vol. 1., pp. 166–67.

Chapter 6: Early Days on the Reservation

55. Dodge, *Our Wild Indians*, pp. 280–81.
56. Donald J. Berthrong, *The Cheyenne and Arapaho Ordeal*. Norman: University of Oklahoma Press, 1976, p. 26.
57. Quoted in Hyde, *Life and Times of George Bent*, p. 197.
58. Mari Sandoz, *Cheyenne Autumn*. New York: McGraw-Hill, 1953, p. 268.
59. Susan Lobo and Steve Talbot, *Native American Voices: A Reader*. New York: Longman, 1998, p. 174.
60. Moore, *The Cheyenne*, p. 273.
61. Moore, *The Cheyenne*, p. 270.
62. Debo, *A History of the Indians of the United States,* p. 299.
63. Berthrong, *The Cheyenne and Arapaho Ordeal*, p. 182.

Chapter 7: An Elastic Will

64. Remington, *Artist Wanderings Among the Cheyennes*, p. 24.
65. Powell, *Sweet Medicine*, vol. 1, p. 341.
66. Moore, *The Cheyenne*, p. 285.
67. Debo, *A History of the Indians of the United States*, p. 378.
68. Stands in Timber and Liberty, *Cheyenne Memories*, pp. 56–57.
69. Debo, *A History of the Indians of the United States*, p. 346.
70. Moore, *The Cheyenne*, p. 296.
71. Quoted in Gary Massaro and Holly Kurtz, "Sand Creek Stories Live On," *Denver Rocky Mountain News*, November 29, 1999, p. 5A.

For Further Reading

Benjamin Capps, *The Indians*. Alexandria, VA: Time-Life Books, 1973. This broad treatment of the Plains Indians includes much on the Cheyenne. It makes for interesting reading, and the photos and illustrations are superb.

George Bird Grinnell, *Pawnee, Blackfoot, and Cheyenne*. New York: Charles Scribner's Sons, 1961. Includes a thorough treatment of Cheyenne customs, nicely interspersed with Cheyenne folklore. This book by one of the foremost authorities on Cheyenne culture was written specifically for young adults.

Stan Hoig, *The Cheyenne*. New York: Chelsea House Publishers, 1989. An interesting and informative account of the Cheyenne with an emphasis on their relations with other tribes and the white man. By a renowned expert on the Cheyenne.

Sally Lodge, *The Cheyenne*. Vero Beach, FL: Rourke Publications, 1990. A brief treatment of the Cheyenne Indians, Lodge's book is printed in large type with an emphasis on illustrations.

Anita Louise McCormick, *Native Americans and the Reservation in American History*. Springfield, NJ: Enslow Publishers, 1996. This history and explanation of the reservation system is also an excellent abbreviated account of the U.S. struggle to obtain Indian land.

Grace Jackson Penny, *Tales of the Cheyennes*. Cambridge, MA: The Riverside Press, 1953. This is a highly readable and entertaining collection of Cheyenne folk tales, including the story of Sweet Medicine.

Gwen Remington, *The Sioux*. San Diego: Lucent Books, 2000. Offers more information on the struggle of the Northern Cheyenne during Red Cloud's War and the Powder River Campaign.

Works Consulted

Ralph K. Andrist, *The Long Death: The Last Days of the Plains Indians*. New York: Macmillan, 1964. Detailed coverage of the Great Plains Wars, including the Sand Creek Massacre and Dull Knife's saga.

James P. Beckwourth, *The Life and Adventures of James P. Beckwourth*. Edited by Thomas D. Bonner. Lincoln: University of Nebraska Press, 1972. A fantastic and exaggerated account of Beckwourth's experiences as a fur trader in the first half of the eighteenth century, this book is nonetheless both highly entertaining and highly informative.

Donald J Berthrong, *The Cheyenne and Arapaho Ordeal*. Norman: University of Oklahoma Press, 1976. A painstakingly documented book by this top Cheyenne authority, covering the early reservation days.

———, *The Southern Cheyennes*. Norman: University of Oklahoma Press, 1972. A thoroughly documented account of Southern Cheyenne history by one of the top contemporary experts.

Angie Debo, *A History of the Indians of the United States*. Norman: University of Oklahoma Press, 1970. The most authoritative and readable account available on this broad topic.

Richard I. Dodge, *Our Wild Indians*. Hartford: A. D. Worthington and Company, 1883. A colonel in the U.S. military during the Great Plains Wars, Dodge studied the Native Americans around him, particularly the Cheyenne, and documented his research in this book.

George A. Dorsey, *The Cheyenne*. Fairfield, WA: Ye Galleon Press, 1975. This slender volume is devoted to Cheyenne religious ceremonies.

Lewis H. Garrard, *Wah-to-yah and the Taos Trail*. Norman: University of Oklahoma Press, 1955. An incredibly enjoyable book by a young man who was there. Garrard visited the Cheyenne in 1846, shortly before tensions escalated between them and the whites.

George Bird Grinnell, *The Cheyenne Indians, Their History and Ways of Life*, vol. 1. Lincoln: University of Nebraska Press, 1972. Grinnell is generally held to be the foremost anthropological authority on the Cheyenne. Years of research culminated in this highly detailed account of their customs, government, and religion.

E. Adamson Hoebel, *The Cheyennes: Indians of the Great Plains*. New York: Holt, Rinehart and Winston, 1960. This book, by another Cheyenne anthropological expert, is slim, but jam-packed with valuable information.

Stan Hoig, *The Peace Chiefs of the Cheyennes*. Norman: University of Oklahoma Press, 1980. Stan Hoig is a contemporary authority on Cheyenne history, and this book, dealing with the political forces driving the Cheyenne, is one of his best.

George E. Hyde, *Life and Times of George Bent*. Edited and annotated by Savoie Lottinville. Norman: University of Oklahoma Press, 1968. Hyde is one of the most respected authorities on many Great Plains tribes. The manuscript for this book, first written in the 1930s, collected dust at the Denver Public Library for over three decades before being rediscovered. Since its publication, this first-person account of the Cheyenne Wars has become an integral source for all Cheyenne historical literature.

Susan Lobo and Steve Talbot, *Native American Voices: A Reader*. New York: Longman, 1998. A college textbook anthology of serious issues facing Native Americans, past and present.

Gary Massaro and Holly Kurtz, "Sand Creek Stories Live On," *Denver Rocky Mountain News*, November 29, 1999. An article regarding the 135th anniversary of the Sand Creek Massacre.

James A. Mooney, *Memoirs of the American Anthropological Association*, vol. 1. New York: Kraus Reprint Corporation, 1964. An excellent short treatment of Cheyenne ways and history by yet another highly respected anthropologist.

John H. Moore, *The Cheyenne*. Cambridge, MA: Blackwell Publishers, 1996. Moore is probably one of the top three contemporary experts on the Cheyenne, their origins, plains lifestyle, history, and reservation life. This is his latest book on the subject.

Luther North, *Man of the Plains*. Edited by Donald F. Danker. Lincoln: University of Nebraska Press, 1961. A fascinating account of Captain Luther North's experiences leading the Pawnee Scouts against the Sioux and Cheyenne in the 1860s and 1870s.

Peter J. Powell, *Sweet Medicine*, vols. 1, 2. Norman: University of Oklahoma Press, 1969. Father Powell spent several years with the Northern Cheyenne in Montana. This massive two-volume work primarily addresses Cheyenne religion and history.

Frederic Remington, *On the Apache Indian Reservation and Artist Wanderings Among the Cheyennes*. Palmer Lake, CO: The Filter Press, 1974. This reprint of an 1891 article in *Century Magazine* is an entertaining and forthright account of Western author and artist Frederic Remington's visit to the Southern Cheyenne.

Frank Gilbert Roe, *The Indian and His Horse*. Norman: University of Oklahoma Press, 1955. From the Indians' first encounter with the horse in the fifteenth century to its use in the last Indian Wars, this book covers the horse's dissemination, husbandry in Indian hands, and influence.

Mari Sandoz, *Cheyenne Autumn*. New York: McGraw-Hill, 1953. A romanticized account of the saga of Dull Knife and Little Wolf by an acknowledged expert.

John Stands in Timber and Margot Liberty, *Cheyenne Memories*. Binghamton, NY: Vail-Ballou Press, 1967. John Stands in Timber was the unofficial tribal historian for the first half of the twentieth century. His memories and those of many Cheyenne elders are recounted in this very readable book.

Reuben Gold Thwaites, ed., *Original Journals of the Lewis and Clark Expedition, 1804–1806*, vol. 1. New York: Arno, 1969. Includes the meticulously kept journals of Meriwether Lewis and William Rogers Clark during their exploration of the Louisiana Territory and the Pacific Northwest, as well as the journals of other members of the party, and their correspondence with Washington, D.C.

Robert M. Utley, *The Indian Frontier of the American West: 1846–1890*. Albuquerque: University of New Mexico Press, 1984. Covers government Indian policy throughout the wars for the Great Plains from 1846 to 1890, from the beginnings of the westward movement to the confinement of all tribes to reservations.

Elliot West, *The Contested Plains: Indians, Goldseekers, and the Rush to Colorado*. Lawrence: The University Press of Kansas, 1998. An interesting, fast-paced account of the forces leading up to and following the fight for the central plains.

Index

Picture Credits

Cover Photo: © Brian Vikander / Corbis
Archive Photos, 41, 61
© Bettmann/Corbis, 33, 48, 64, 81
Corbis, 25, 45, 49, 66, 67, 70
Denver Public Library, 9, 11, 15, 16, 18, 19, 22, 23, 27, 28, 32, 36,
    40, 43, 56, 58, 59, 63, 69, 72, 73, 77, 78
© Medford Historical Society Collection/Corbis, 53
© Richard T. Nowitz/Corbis, 29
Stock Montage, 38, 44, 47, 74
© Underwood and Underwood/Corbis, 14
© Brian Vikander/Corbis, 13, 65

About the Author

Gwen Remington is a freelance writer who has published fiction and nonfiction pieces in several horse magazines. In 1997 she graduated magna cum laude from the University of Sioux Falls, earning her B.A. in English. In 1998 she obtained her M.A., also in English. Remington, a native of North Dakota, has lived most of her life on the Great Plains. She currently resides in Cheyenne, Wyoming, where she is working on a book about the Pawnee. Her first book, *The Sioux*, was also published by Lucent Books.